WILLIAM BAER

The Gravedigger

A Romance by William Baer

ISBN-13: 978-1-962168-49-6

Praise for William Baer's Fiction:

"...storytelling at its best."—Joseph Pearce

"...mesmerizing, engrossing, and delectable."—Terri Brown-Davidson

"...brilliant and profoundly affecting."—Samuel Maio

"...the reader is irrevocably hooked."—Angela Alaimo O'Donnell

"...perfect pacing, stunning imagery, complex characterization."—Hollis Seamon

"...a can't-put-it-down thrill ride."—*Publishers Weekly* (Five-star review)

"...captivating, thought-provoking, and multi-layered."—*Reading Café* (Five-star review)

"...the writing is crisp, sarcastic, and wryly funny."—*Foreword Reviews* (Five-star review)

"...I love books like this! A rarity. Five Stars!"—*Reader Views* (Five-star review)

For my family and friends

"O my Luve's like a sweet, sweet chocolate."

– Angus Kinnell

1. Chocolate

Friday, October 23rd

It started with chocolate.

Naturally.

I was cutting across the South Lawn on the Columbia campus at Morningside Heights. Walking across the grass between Low Library, where they handed me a diploma four years ago, and Butler Library with its two million books. I was, of course, listening to music, but not what you might expect from a twenty-five-year-old. It was a playlist of old Gaelic songs once recorded by my father, including *"Mo Rùn Gàidhealach,"* which means "My Highland Love," which my father composed over thirty years ago.

Bidh mo ghaol-sa dhi buan am feasda
Air Eilean àluinn a' Cheò.

Meaning something like:

I will love my love forever and ever
On the beautiful Island of Skye.

Little did I know, 3,000 miles away, at that very moment, my father was singing the exact same song over the cliffs at Tarskavaig on the Island of Skye. Right above my mother's grave. Beneath a brilliant Skeat sunset at 5:30 Scot time.

Back here in Manhattan, it was only 12:30, on a lovely, crisp, October afternoon. I was dressed in a blue-plaid skirt, a button-up yellow blouse, and a double-breasted blue Lauren blazer with gold buttons. Looking perfectly professional for my presentation on 114th Street.

"There are four basic food groups."

They waited without interest.

I continued.

"Milk chocolate, dark chocolate, white chocolate, and chocolate truffles."

They smiled creepy little "I'm craving sweets" smiles.

There were twelve of them, all five-year-olds, all twitching weirdly in their seats. It was Rickie's kindergarten class, and I was there to lighten the afternoon with my "expertise."

"Chocolate was once known as 'the food of the gods.'" I explained. "It makes us happy, reduces stress, and gives us energy. It's one of the most perfect things on earth. Like snowflakes, roses, diamonds, baseball, and love."

They nodded politely, ignoring most of what I was saying.

"It's also good for your heart" I tried, "and good for your blood pressure."

Which was perfectly dumb. What five-year-old cares about his blood pressure? I wondered what my father would do.

I leaned over them and smiled.

Intimately.

Conspiratorially.

"I have only one rule about eating chocolate. Would you like to hear it?"

They were slightly interested.

"Never eat more chocolate than you can lift."

They liked it.

They actually smiled. I had them back. Rickie also smiled in the back of her colorfully-decorated classroom, clearly relieved that I was no longer boring her "brats" to death.

I pressed forward.

"I tell you what, kids, let's do some math!"

Which revived disinterest.

"How do you get two pounds of chocolate home from the store in a hot car? So the chocolate won't melt?"

They had no idea, but they appreciated the difficulty of the situation.

"You eat it in the parking lot."

Rickie rolled her eyes, but two of the kids clapped.

My favorite students.

Yes, I was shamelessly playing to the crowd. Any semblance of a real "lesson" was long gone, but I felt fully justified since I'd already discussed the history and geography of chocolate, as well as how it's made. All to drowsy eyes.

"All right, kids, any questions? Comments?"

One little boy felt it necessary to express his deepest feelings.

"I like chocolate without nuts."

"Me too!" I agreed. "Nuts just take up space where there could be more chocolate."

This garnered general approval.

Then a little girl, a little blondie who was much too pretty for her own good, raised her hand.

"My father says sweets aren't healthy."

"Well, you father's correct about most sweets, but not about chocolate. It's a vegetable."

They all looked shocked.

"Chocolate is made from cocoa beans, and the sugar comes from sugar cane, which is also a plant. Besides, if it's milk chocolate, then it's full of nutritious milk."

This time they *all* clapped.

I was on a roll.

A little redhead boy raised his hand.

"Do they *really* pay you money to taste chocolate?"

A teacherly voice, thick with the Bronx, called out from the back of the classroom.

"Yes, they do, Eddie. And very good money I might add."

They looked at me intently. A little brunette expressed the group sentiment.

"I think you're the luckiest person in the world."

They all nodded.

They all wanted my job.

"I think I am too," I agreed.

But blondie smarty-pants had more to say.

"Then why'd your boyfriend dump you?"

I was stunned.

"Dump?" I said stupidly.

A cell vibrated in the back of the classroom. I was hoping that Rickie would rescue me, but, instead, she gestured that she needed to take the call outside, stood up, and immediately slipped out the door. Leaving me alone with her twelve little monsters.

I flashed back to *Lord of the Flies*.

Then a sweet little boy tried to clarify the situation.

"Miss Moreno said to be extra nice to you since your boyfriend dumped you. Since you still aren't over it."

Miss Moreno, my best friend, would be strangled later.

I did my best.

"The truth is, kids, I *am* over it. Thank goodness. Unfortunately, things like that happen in life. But I'll tell you another secret."

A potential escape hatch.

They seemed curious.

"Many people believe that eating chocolate can heal a broken heart."

"Can it?" asked a serious little munchkin.

"Yes, I believe it can."

Rickie re-entered the room, and I gave her a mock glare.

"Have they been causing trouble?" she asked.

"No, just the teacher."

2. Córdoba's

Friday, October 23rd

Later, after a quick browse at Westsider Books, we hopped in a cab.

"Córdoba's on 116th," I said.

Rickie was surprised.

"I finally dump the brats, and you want to go to Córdoba's?"

"You really like that word 'dump.'"

She ignored me.

"Why are we going to Córdoba's? You're supposed to be over Matt."

"I *am* over Matt, which you can announce to your class by the way. I'm leaving town for two weeks tomorrow, and I want to eat at my favorite restaurant. Besides, who likes Mexican food more than me? Besides, let's not forget that Córdoba's was *my* favorite restaurant long before I took Matt there."

She changed the subject.

"What's the book?"

I took it out of the bag and handed it over. She read the title:

The Highland MacDonalds: A History of the Scottish Highlands

She looked at me.

"I thought you knew all this stuff?"

"I do, but I like to remind myself."

She smiled wishfully.

"I wish *I* was going to Scotland!"

"You wish you were going anywhere!"

Inside the colorful restaurant, Rickie checked the reservation with the maître d'. A comforting mariachi was playing over the speakers as I looked around and saw what I didn't want to see.

Immediately, I started across the floor of the restaurant, in between the crowded tables, and I could hear Rickie behind me.

"Uh-oh!"

I stopped at a table with a young couple. Matt and a pretty snowbunny.

"What the hell are you doing here?"

I don't really have much of a temper, but I was mad.

Angry.

"It's good to see you, Polly."

His sincerity was a bit unnerving, so Rickie took over.

"You've really got a nerve coming here, Matt."

He seemed helpless.

"I'm sorry."

He then commenced the most awkward introduction in world history.

"This is Kimberly Sinclair, and this is Polly Kinnell and Rickie Moreno."

The rest of us, the three women, just looked at each other. Then Kimberly turned to Matt.

"Why'd you dump her? She's beautiful."

Am I?

It was suddenly very hard not to appreciate Kimberly, who, I have to admit, was remarkably pretty.

So maybe it's time for a few facts about The Chocolate Princess:

> Once upon a time (I hope this is the way you want your story), the Chocolate Princess was born in the wilds of New Jersey, in a place called Scotch Plains, to a wonderful mother and father. The father was an immigrant from Scotland and a chocolate maker. A Chocolatier. He owned Kinnell's Chocolates, a boutique shop on Fifth near Saks. The mother, Bonnie MacDonald Kinnell, also an immigrant from the Island of Skye, was a librarian, an amateur Scot historian, and a marvelous mother.
>
> The CP (Chocolate Princess), also known as Polly Kinnell, had no brothers or sisters, but

she grew up happily in the wilds of New Jersey. Eventually, she commuted to Columbia University in Manhattan, where she majored in British literature, with a special interest in Scottish ballads, Burns, Scott, and Stevenson, with a minor in something called business. Ever since she was a young girl, she'd helped her father with the store on Fifth Avenue, developing a reputation for chocolate "tasting."

She also had a "secret" ambition. Or ambitions. She wanted to write a book about the extraordinary history of chocolate, maybe for children, maybe for adults. But she also wanted to write stories of the kind she'd read as a child with her mother. Stories about life, about fate, about love. But all such ambitions were eventually put on hold, although she did keep writing late some nights, writing extensive Amazon reviews of new and old books whenever she could find the time.

Which no one knew about except her father.

In her junior year, she moved into the city, sharing an apartment on 119th Street with her best friend Rickie. Where they both still live. When her mother died, when the CP was twenty-one, her father moved back to Scotland, to Armadale on Skye, opening a second Kinnell's Chocolates, leaving the one on Fifth in the less capable hands of his daughter and his kindly sister, Aunt Katie MacDonald, a widow. But the father, Angus James Kinnell, came back to visit the CP several times a year, and was always inviting Polly to travel to the Highlands, which she wanted to do, but invariably put off, until guilt finally overwhelmed her and she arranged for a two-week vacation in Skye beginning tomorrow night.

(Since this story, as you've requested, is a "romance"), then, yes, there *was* a romance between the Chocolate Princess and the legendary Ice Warrior for almost two years until he dumped her a year ago, who was now, rather sheepishly, sitting beside his gorgeous snowbunny, staring upward at the Chocolate Princess, above his waiting fajitas and salted margherita.

Where were we?

Oh, yeah, Kimberly had just said that I was beautiful.

"You're not so bad yourself, sister," Rickie responded, "but he'll dump you too."

Always the word "dump."

Kimberly (let's start calling her Kim) was not only undaunted but oddly amenable to the possibility.

"Maybe he will."

She looked back at me.

"It's best not to take these big-shot athletes too seriously."

I didn't know what to make of that.

As for Matt, he seemed nonplussed, staring at his date.

"You're a big help!"

I'd had enough.

I'd already made my grand entrance, attracting too much attention from the other diners, and now it was time for a gracious but equally grand exit.

"You shouldn't have come here, Matt," I said.

It was restrained.

It was true.

I turned around and started walking away, hearing Rickie behind me.

Getting in the last word, as always.

"Try the Juárez jalapeños, Matt. They'll blow your brains out."

3. Rooftop

Friday, October 23rd

I was staring at the smoke.

There was a huge, dangerous-looking cloud of smoke rising from the rooftop into the evening sky over the greatest city in the world.

"How can you be so stupid?"

It was a rhetorical question, but Rickie kept going anyway.

"He was looking for *you*! I'll bet he was down at the shop earlier. Check with your aunt. I think he's snooping around again."

Since we'd left Córdoba's with nothing to eat, not even an enchilada, Rickie decided to burn the daylights out of some sausages on her rooftop grill, clearly impervious to the cloud of smoke.

Maybe Rickie was right about Matt.

"Well, he can go snoop somewhere else."

I sounded like one of her kindergarteners.

"Actually," she decided, "he's really not so bad,

Polly. Why don't guys like that chase after me?"

"Whenever they do, you run them off."

She ignored me.

"Isn't that too much smoke?"

She ignored me again.

The door to the roof opened, and her father came toward us. He was carrying a small gift-wrapped package and a large grocery bag full of long loaves of Italian bread. He was still in uniform.

"Hey, dad!" Rickie yelled out.

She loved her father like I loved my father.

Two daddy's girls.

Maybe it's Rickie time:

> The Italian Bombshell (I made that one up, I hope you like it) was *born* in the Bronx, *sounded* like the Bronx, and *carried* the Bronx with her everywhere she went. She was Italian-American, looked Italian, sounded Italian. She's twenty-five, my age, shortish, adorable, with big brown eyes, cropped dark hair, and a perfectly trim figure. As you've probably noticed, she's good-hearted, honest to a fault, hyper-blunt, always shooting from the hip, and smart as a whip. She prefers jeans and sweatshirts but can dress up nicely if she wants to. She was *magna cum laude* at Columbia, majoring in Italian history, minoring in education.
>
> She runs the Kangaroo Kindergarten on

114th Street, will do *anything* for the little kids she calls "brats," and hopes to open another kindergarten in the near future. "You need to get the brats off on the right foot. Get them ready to learn."

She's also the best friend in the universe.

"Smells great, honey. Here's the bread."

Then he sees the smoke.

"Is that legal?"

"You're the cop," his daughter countered.

I felt the urge to make a statement.

"I've been expecting the fire department, not the police department."

The two Moreno's gave me a *que será, será* shrug.

Then Mr. Moreno looked down at me, sitting on my silly lawn chair, away from the conflagration.

"Hey, sweetheart."

He always called me "sweetheart."

Just like my dad.

"Why don't you stay for supper," I suggested. "There might even be some sausages left when your pyro daughter finishes setting the neighborhood on fire."

"I can't. I've got to get back to the Bronx. Rickie's mom's got something special going on."

"Name it old man," Rickie called out.

"Baked ziti, pasta fasul."

"Both?" I wondered.

"Both."

"Why did I leave the Bronx?" Rickie lamented.

Then her dad handed me the wrapped package, obviously a book, and he sat down in Rickie's lawn chair.

"It was leaning on the door downstairs."

I had a feeling about what it might be, and I didn't want to open it.

Rickie wasn't having any of it.

"Open it!"

Which I did, then I handed the book to Rickie's dad who read the title out loud, so his daughter could hear:

Scottish Ghost Stories

"Flip to the title page," Rickie told her old man, "then read it out loud."

Which he did:

"From Matt, with love."

He was surprised.

"Are you two back together?"

"Definitely not."

He looked confused.

So his big-mouth daughter tried to help.

"Guess who popped up at Córdoba's?"

Her father understood, looking at me.

"Is that why you're eating charcoal sausages?"

Before I was forced to answer, a head popped up at the south end of the roof. Looking over the little ledge that ran around the edge of the roof. It was the head of Hector Hernandez, the building's fiftyish, world-weary superintendent. He was obviously standing on the fire escape ladder. With only his frazzled head visible. I felt certain he was wearing his ubiquitous brown work clothes and tool belt. He seemed impervious to the fact that he was dangling six stories in the air.

"That's too much smoke, Rickie! That can't be legal."

She was undaunted.

"It's *perfectly* legal. Right, dad?"

It was clear that Sergeant Anthony Moreno preferred not to lie, so his daughter cut him off.

"Just tell Mr. Hernandez that everything's all right, so he can go downstairs and fix the light in the hallway."

Hector Hernandez looked at Anthony Moreno, but neither one said a word.

Then Rickie ripped off a piece of Italian bread and dipped it in the tomato sauce simmering at the edge of the grill far from the sausages. Then she stepped over to the edge of the roof and put it (shoved it) into the mouth of the disembodied head.

Which he ate.

With pleasure.

"That's a clever bribe, Rickie, just don't burn

down the building."

He looked over at me.

"You have a great trip, Polly!"

"Thanks, Hector."

Then his head was gone, and I started thumbing through the book.

"There's Duntulm Castle."

I held up the picture for Mr. Moreno.

"It's nothing but ruins these days, but I can't wait to see it. It's where my dad proposed to my mom, and he'll be taking me there the day after tomorrow."

Rickie stepped over to take a look.

"Ghosts?" she asked.

"Of course."

"How's your dad doing over there?" her dad asked about the other dad.

"Great. He's happy to be back home."

When Rickie went back to her grill, her phone rang. Then her dad stood up to leave.

"You know," I told him, "I've never been to Skye."

He was surprised.

"I thought you went over there."

"My parents took me to Scotland when I was thirteen. We went to Edinburgh and St. Andrews and Loch Ness and Culloden, but there was an emergency back home with Aunt Katie, so we never got to the islands in the Highlands."

"Well, sweetheart, have a fantastic time."

He kissed me on the top of the head, waved to his daughter, and left the roof.

Eventually, Rickie came over and sat down in the lawn chair beside me.

She was oddly subdued.

There were tears in her eyes.

"It was your aunt. She asked me to tell you."

She took my hands in hers.

"Your dad died this afternoon. He was at the cemetery visiting your mother."

4. Cemetery

Monday, October 26th

Réquiem aetérnam *dona ei, Dòmine.*

I was dressed in black, and my world was black.
Everything was overcast.
With lingering fog.
I stared at the coffin, trying not to imagine that my father was inside. I was supported by Rickie and surrounded by people I didn't know. My poor Aunt Katie was so overcome with the loss that she was unable to make the transatlantic flight.

My only remaining relative was 3,000 miles away.
There was wafting incense.
There was holy water and signs of the cross, but I was numb to everything.
The priest, assisted by a young altar boy, finished the burial service:

Altar Boy: *Et lux perpétua lúceat ei.*
Priest: *Requiéscat in pace.*
Altar Boy: *Amen.*

I looked away from the coffin, beyond the priest, beyond my mother's headstone, beyond all the other headstones, and stared at the Grim Reaper standing alone and waiting. Patiently. He was leaning on a shovel, not a scythe. He was dressed in work clothes, not black robes. He was also wearing dark black shades on a cloudy morning. Sunglasses on a sunless day! Some stupid callous gravedigger who couldn't wait to shove my father into his grave and shovel dirt on his face.

The piper started. I think it was *Amazing Grace.* Maybe it was *Loch Lomond* or *Scotland the Brave.* What difference did it make?

He'd collapsed right here. High on the cliffs above Loch a' Ghlinne in Tarskavaig Cemetery. Singing at the grave of his one true love, singing the song he'd once written just for her.

Heart failure.

Somehow, the kindest heart in the world had somehow failed and left me all alone.

Angus James Kinnell. Born in Brogaig in the Highlands in northern Skye. A Scot "Kinnell" of the MacDonald clan, with not a drop of Irish. Who spoke Gaelic, taught me a bit, and wrote songs in the old language. Who was well-known in the Highlands as a powerful singer of Gaelic songs, who then apprenticed as a chocolatier, then brought his chocolates to America. Who, knowing nothing about New York City, bought a home in Scotch Plains, New Jersey, twenty-eight miles from Rockefeller Center. Surely there had to be some Scots in a place called "Scotch" Plains?

Which was actually founded by Scots in 1684, and played a significant role in the Battle of Short Hills, June 1777, when General William Howe tried to dupe George Washington by feigning an evacuation to Staten Island then wheeling around, attempting to catch the rebels off-guard. 12,000 attempting to crush 8,000. But Washington, lurking in the Watchung Mountains over Scotch Plains knew that they were coming, and he drove them back. Being yet another "stalemate" that was really a victory for the outnumbered rebels.

So my father moves to a place called Scotch Plains, a lovely little town, quaint and family-friendly, with over a hundred historic homes and buildings, some with underground tunnels for runaway slaves. With at least twenty homes that predate the Revolution. With a "downtown" that's three blocks long. With the famous Stage House Inn, where Lafayette once stayed. With no supermarket.

But it wasn't a Scot haven anymore. Actually, it was mostly Italian, and he loved it there, as did my mother, as did I. It was a wonderful place to grow up. But in my mother's heart, within my father's heart, there was always a longing for home. For the

Highlands, for the Island of Skye, for their heritage, for the place they'd fallen in love. The "enchanted" island of mists and history and Celtic culture, and now I was finally standing in the midst of it, feeling absolutely nothing.

Nothing but regret, nothing but guilt.

Ashamed that I'd never come before. That I'd never come to visit my father before his heart had failed and before my heart had been broken into a million meaningless pieces. Before he'd collapsed into death. Before everything seemed meaningless.

It was over.

A long line of solemn-faced people offered well-intentioned commiserations. None of which I heard. Eventually, Rickie managed to get me away, into the back of the black limousine, as the crowd gradually dispersed. I sat there, impervious to everything, staring mindlessly out the window at the old cemetery.

Then I saw him again.

I lowered the window.

He was kneeling at the edge of my father's grave. Maybe he was praying. Which I found particularly irritating. Who the hell was *he* to be praying at my father's grave. The man who was about to cover him with dirt.

5. Kinnell's Chocolates

Wednesday, October 28th

Rickie flipped on the lights, and we stepped inside.

I looked around.

"I should be happy here. I'm surrounded by chocolate."

I was talking to myself, but I didn't mind that Rickie could hear me. We were standing in my father's chocolate shop in Armadale, close to Armadale Castle, on the Sleat peninsula at the southern end of Skye. I'd only seen pictures of the store before, and like the Fifth Avenue store, it was impeccable. Like my father. Dark woods, with endless glass/mahogany displays of every kind of chocolate imaginable:

Creams, clusters, cherries, drops, cups, truffles, rolls, patties, mousse, fudge, mocha, crème brûlée, mint, butter crunch, walnut, almond, coconut, nonpareils, marshmallow, caramel, cherries, and my favorite, milk chocolate squares.

With a "Closed" sign on the front door.

Rickie ignored me.

"It's lovely."

She was charmed, and, let's face it, not much "charms" the girl from the Bronx.

"Yes, it is."

"Angus made a lot of people happy here. With all his chocolates."

She looked at me, then finished her thought.

"In all kinds of ways."

Meaning his kindnesses.

She spotted the milk chocolate.

"Can I?"

"Of course. I'll have to sell off most of the inventory. Maybe I can ship a few things back to my aunt. It kills me to shut the place down. I wish I could keep it going somehow."

Rickie popped a square into her mouth.

Then smiled.

"What did Fred Astaire say? 'I'm in Heaven.'"

I tried to smile, and she tried to help me.

"You know what my best friend once told me?"

"I bet I do."

"She told me that there's nothing better than a best friend, except for a best friend who likes chocolate."

I managed to smile. It felt rather pathetic.

Rickie was making plans.

"This place is making me hungry. Let's eat at the

pub tonight. I'm sick of eating at the cottage."

I hesitated.

"I'm not sure if I should."

"Why not? We buried your dad two days ago. I'm sure it's OK to go out and have a bite to eat."

I wasn't convinced.

She went over to the window.

"Wow! Look at that sunset!"

"Skye sunsets are famous."

She turned back to me.

"It's very beautiful here, Polly. No wonder your dad came back after your mother died."

"Yeah."

"He had four good years, right?"

"Right."

I changed the subject.

"You go get the car; I'll lock the place down."

She could tell that I wanted to be alone, and she left without a word. I sat down on a lonely wooden bench and stared at the sunset over the mountains. Over the Cullin. Lots of brilliant reds and streaking yellows.

Yes, I knew that I was whining a lot. At least, in my heart. After all, I was a daddy's girl, and I knew it. A few years ago, Rickie called me a "daddy's girl," so I looked it up. I wasn't sure if it was supposed to be a good thing or a bad thing. I learned that it's either/or. The bad dad spoils his daughter, shirks discipline, and "shows her off." As a consequence, the daughter spends her entire life seeking out daddy's attention and approval, trying to be whatever he wants her to be. She becomes self-absorbed, insecure, immature, and narcissistic. She lacks empathy and never grows up. She finds the real world to be a dark and intolerant place, which never appreciates her like her father does. Life is unfair, and she wants her daddy to rescue her from her problems.

Sometimes, there's even a weirdo "flirtatiousness" to the relationship, with creepy sexual overtones. Which I'd rather not discuss.

But the good father, like *my* father, is a loving disciplinarian, who always cares, always supports, always models an honest and upright behavior. That was Angus Kinnell. It's said that these kinds of daughters grow up to be "grown women," not "grown girls," who accept and challenge life, who can readily distinguish between bogus relationships and the real thing. After all, such a father is the first and most important example of how a relationship with a man should be.

I remember reading somewhere that some therapist claimed that in the course of his entire professional life, "I've met very few women who did not unconsciously or consciously pick a romantic partner based on the characteristics of her father."

Matt Brooks was a kind young man in the mold of my father, but he'd broken the mold when he "dumped" me.

I'm telling you all this, so you can try and fathom

the depth of my sorrow.
     My loneliness.

6. The Sult Inn

Wednesday, October 28th

"Come on, Polly, a little fiddle music won't kill you."

I was sitting in our rental car in a crowded parking lot. We could hear the fiddle in the distance, and Rickie was trying to coax me into the local tavern.

"I don't think I should go inside."

She ignored me.

"Too late! I'm starved, and I'm going inside to get us a table."

I watched her go.

Eventually, I gave up. I locked the car and headed for the front door.

There were several signs at the entrance, but I only read two. The first one said, "No Television." Which was fine with me. The second one said, "No Cell Phone Use Inside the Tavern." Well, I'm hardly a cell phone zombie, but it seemed a bit much.

I opened the front door and stepped inside. Facing

the doorway was a skinny teenage boy sitting on a wooden stool. He smiled a big smile and handed me a small card. Before I had a chance to read it, a couple came over to the door preparing to leave. The boy looked directly at the woman, who was maybe thirty-five or so.

"Come again, when you can't stay so long."

I was stunned by his rudeness.

Then he looked at the man.

"I overheard your conversation."

"Aye, and what'd you think?"

"Empty barrels make the most noise."

It was remarkably obnoxious.

When the couple left, the boy looked directly at me.

"A beautiful woman is a paradise for the eyes."

I was fed up.

"You've got some nerve, little man."

Then I looked around the crowded tavern and saw Rickie waving me over.

The place was old-fashioned, comfortable, with lots of wood, with sawdust on the flagstone floor. Off to the left, raised on a small low stage, was the tavern's fiddle player. He was playing an excellent fiddle. I glanced over. He was lean, and tall, and rugged, maybe thirty years old, dressed in jeans and a burgundy sweater.

Wearing shades!

Shades! Inside, at night!

Great!

The ghoulish gravedigger.

"Polly!"

Rickie was calling from somewhere, so I turned away from the gravedigger and headed in her direction.

Then I saw Matt, who was sitting next to Rickie.

What was *he* doing here?

I definitely wasn't happy about it.

Yeah, sure, he's handsome, and, yeah, sure, he's pretty famous, but I just wished that he'd go away.

Maybe it's time to pause a moment and introduce him a bit better:

> The Ice Warrior, aka Matthew Brooks, is a world-class speedskater who grew up in Ann Arbor, skated at Black Lake, then went to the University of Wisconsin. Two years ago, at the age of twenty-four, he won the 500m gold at the Pyeongchang Olympics in South Korea, setting a new world record. He was now training, mostly in Milwaukee, for the next Olympics in Beijing.
>
> Did I mention he's handsome? Much like the legendary skater Dan Jansen, the Ice Warrior was tall, powerfully built, and equally handsome. Think Chris Pine. (If Chris Pine was a world-class athlete and the winner of the prestigious Sullivan Award.) As a result, the IW (Ice Warrior) was constantly pursued by every

snowbunny and ice angel in the entire wide universe. At one time, he did have a romance of sorts with the Chocolate Princess, but being a complete moron, he terminated the relationship. Now he's come to Scotland to irritate her even more.

I stepped over to the table.

"What are *you* doing here?"

"I came to pay my respects. I'm sorry about your dad."

He couldn't have been more polite, but I couldn't have cared less.

"Do you want me to leave?" he asked.

There was a waitress standing next to the table. I looked at her tray.

"Is that a Talisker?"

"Yes, a double."

"Perfect."

I picked it up, right off her tray, and drained it. It burned my inners like a hot poker, and it felt great.

"Get me another."

The waitress nodded and left, probably glad to get away from me.

I sat down between Rickie and Matt and things got a bit hazy. I think I cried a bit. I'm not sure.

When the second Talisker arrived, I gulped it down. Or was it the third? I started crying again, and the music stopped, and I looked at the fiddler who was looking at me. With his stupid shades. With what looked like concern on his face.

But I didn't want his concern.

I'd had enough. I stood up.

"Why'd you stop, fiddle-boy? And why are you staring at me?"

I have a suspicion that everyone in the pub was also staring at me, but I didn't care.

Not in the least.

The fiddle guy said nothing, which was even more irritating.

"Who the hell are you anyway? Standing there with your stupid shovel. You couldn't wait to throw dirt on his face, could you? And, oh yeah, who are *you* to be praying at his grave?"

The place went silent. Maybe it already was. Rickie pulled on my sweater.

"Sit down, knucklehead, you're making a scene."

"Good!"

I looked back at the shovel-man.

"And what's with the shades, pal? It's nighttime."

I looked around, at all the staring eyes.

"And what *is* this place anyway? And who's that little jerk at the front door insulting everyone?"

For some reason, that particular comment got a rise out of the crowd.

Unhappy murmurs.

Then the fiddle guy said something in Gaelic, with the thickest brogue I'd ever heard, and the place went silent again. Yeah, I studied Gaelic with my mother, but I was too upset to understand a word of it.

Rickie stood up.

"We're leaving!"

"The hell we are!"

Which is all I remember.

I was soon engulfed in a warm and wonderful whiskey blackness.

7. Polly

Wednesday, October 28th

[Since I was unconscious at the time, overdosed on the hard alcohols of Talisker's whiskey, this section of the story is told from the p.o.v. of Ian MacIan, the Graveyard Knight, who told me these details about two months later on my first trip to Inverness.]

We were sitting on the steps outside the pub.

Me, Jimmy, and the Yank.

Everyone else had gone home, and we were decompressing.

After the "incident."

"What's the deal?" the Yank wondered.

He'd just read the little white card.

"It's an old tradition here," I explained. "The locals love it. So do the tourists."

"Except one."

"Except one."

He held up the card.

"I guess she never read it. It says right here, if you don't want an insult on the way out, all you have to do is raise your hand."

"Which is easy enough."

"Any other disasters?"

"Never anything like tonight."

Matt looked at Jimmy. I liked the Yank. I liked the way he treated Jimmy. Like he was one of the boys.

"Give me some of your favorites?"

Jimmy obliged.

"You're the kind of person who lights up a room by leaving it."

The Yank liked that one a lot, so Jimmy continued.

"I believe you dove into the low end of the gene pool when the lifeguard wasn't looking."

The Yank smiled again.

"If brains were taxed, you'd get a rebate."

"Don't encourage him," I kidded. "He knows thousands."

Like everyone else, I guess Matt Brooks was trying to "figure out" Jimmy.

"You got quite the memory, kid."

Jimmy gave him a nod, then Matt looked at me.

"One of the waitresses said you're planning to open another pub in New York."

"The owners are," I explained. "Do you think it would work over there?"

"I do."

He looked up at the large sign over the front door.

The Sult Inn

"I didn't get it at first, but I like it," he decided. "The Sult Inn. 'Insult.' Get a compliment on the way in and an insult on the way out. Who came up with that?"

"Who knows. We Scots are always coming up with stuff."

I definitely liked the guy. You never know about big-shot athletes, but he seemed very regular. Truly unpretentious.

He wanted to make something perfectly clear.

"You know, she's not really like that. Not at all. Actually, she's quite wonderful, but she's out of her mind with grief. I hope you guys can understand that."

We did.

"She was close to her father. *Very* close. Back when we were dating, she used to talk about him all the time."

"What happened?"

It was Jimmy.

Matt seemed a bit surprised, but he answered the question.

"Well, I'll tell you what happened, Jimmy. I was a damned fool. The training was wearing me down, and we didn't get to see each other as much as we wanted, and there was a pretty girl on the circuit that I got to like, so I put an end to it. It was the biggest mistake I've ever made in my life."

"You want her back?" I asked.

"Yes, and I'm off to a great start."

"When she sobers up, she'll appreciate the fact that you came all the way over here to pay your respects."

"I hope so."

He looked at Jimmy again.

"Guess where I met her?"

Jimmy shrugged.

"At the New York Chocolate Festival. It was after a meet at Lake Placid, and I had two days to spend in New York City before heading back to Milwaukee. But I'd never been to New York before, and I was a bit overwhelmed, and I had no idea what to do. Then some guy at the hotel told me about the 'Big Chocolate Show.' So after taking the ferry around the Statue of Liberty, I went to the Terminal Warehouse on Eleventh Avenue, and I wandered around, amid hundreds of exhibitors and all kinds of demonstrations and panel discussions, and there she was in the 'Kinnell's Manhattan' booth, and she offered me a sample of chocolate. It was perfect, and so was she."

"I like chocolate," Jimmy said.

Something we could all agree about.

Matt grew pensive.

"Someday, when all this 'fame' stuff is over, I'll be an anonymous skating coach somewhere, and my medals and trophies won't mean a thing."

I tried to be encouraging.

"They're still something to be proud of."

Jimmy tossed out a seeming non-sequitur.

"33.95."

Matt was amazed. He looked at Jimmy.

"How do you know that?"

It was Matt's time in the 500 at the last Olympics. The current world record.

Jimmy shrugged.

I helped.

"He's a fan."

It seemed hard to believe.

"He's a speedskating fan?"

"Yes. He knows all the world records. From 1891 to the present. In every event."

It seemed impossible.

Curious, the Yank threw out some names.

"Jeremy Wotherspoon."

"34.03, 2007."

"Dan Jansen."

"35.76, 1994."

Uwe-Jens Mey."

"36.43, 1992."

The Yank was stunned.

"You know my sport better than me!"

When Jimmy said nothing, Matt looked at me.

"How come?"

"A friend got us interested during the last Olympics."

I left it right there, and he thought it over. He'd come 3,500 miles from Milwaukee to Skye and run into two skate fans at an "insult" pub.

He looked back at Jimmy.

"I'll tell you something, Jimmy. It's a lot less stressful racing those races, than trying to get back with Polly Kinnell."

Jimmy, who was now the Yank's romance consultant, said nothing.

"What about you guys?" Matt wondered.

Jimmy just smiled his perpetual smile, so Matt checked back with me.

"I've been steering clear."

He seemed surprised.

"No girlfriend at all?"

"Not for a long time."

"Is that a good idea?"

I didn't have a good answer.

8. Kinnell House

Thursday, October 29th

My eyes popped opened.

As best they could.

I was waking from a stupor.

Which seemed like a good name for it.

Onomatopoeic.

My father once said that the word stupor was a combination of "stupid" and "oops."

Whatever it was, my head was killing me and my whole body ached. Then I started to remember last night, and things got a thousand times worse. Was it just a dream? An ugly nightmare?

I sat up, unsteadily, on the edge of the bed and did the only thing I could think of.

"Rickie!"

Maybe she could make it go away.

Eventually, the door opened and Rickie came in, dressed in jeans with a Columbia sweatshirt. Looking totally refreshed. Looking eager to enjoy another wonderful new day.

"What did I do?"

"What didn't you do?"

"Tell me it's not true."

"I'm not a lying kind of friend."

"Then tell me the truth."

"Fine. You made a perfect fool of yourself. You disgraced the entire United States of America, and I'm certain that every American tourist is now banned from the island."

She seemed to be enjoying herself.

"How could I behave like that?"

It was time for a little compassion.

"I guess the anger had to come out sometime, hon. Unfortunately, you had to do it in public."

I was mortified.

"What *was* that weird place?"

"A bar with a gimmick. When you enter, they hit you with a compliment, and when you leave, they give you an insult. Apparently it's very popular with American tourists, excepting, of course, Miss Polly Kinnell."

More came back.

"Who was that strange little boy?"

"A local kid. Mentally damaged somehow, but he's apparently a savant of some kind, with an incredible memory. He's perfectly harmless and very popular on the island. He's actually a bit older than he looks."

"He looks fourteen."

"He's seventeen."

The rest of it came back in a rush.

"Did I really yell at the gravedigger."

"Yes, with an exquisite cruelty that I never knew you were capable of."

"And Matty?"

"Yeah, the poor guy comes all the way over here to get insulted. At the Sult Inn!"

She laughed at her little joke, which I didn't "get" until later.

I shook my head.

What else could I do?

"Thank God we're leaving tomorrow night," I said. "I'm afraid to show my face around here."

She sat down next to me, on the edge of the bed, and put her arm around me.

"People understand, Polly. Besides the fiddle guy said something in Gaelic that seemed to calm everyone down."

She hugged me tight.

"What came over me?"

"Grief. And several double-whiskies."

"First my mom, now my dad. I miss them so much."

"They're in a good place, Polly. And they're together."

It wasn't much comfort.

"I'm going to the graveyard in the morning to say

goodbye."

"Should I come?"

"I think I should go alone."

She didn't disagree.

"Fine, but don't forget this nutty weather. Bring an umbrella."

9. Cemetery

Friday, October 30th

"The Island of Mist."

Which sounds very "enchanting" and highly "romantic," until it gets so thick you can't see out the front window of your rental car. Then it turns to rain. Then you arrive at a completely saturated graveyard where you get your Camry stuck in the disgusting mud. So you spin your wheels for a while until you give up, then you pull out your cell for a rescue call. But the phone's dead, because somebody, naturally, forgot to charge the stupid thing. So you sit in your trapped car and stare at the tombstones through the falling sheets of the tempest, and you say to yourself, the hell with it, I'm not giving up, I'm saying goodbye to my mother and my father no matter what. A little rain won't kill me. So I reach for my umbrella, but it's not there.

Then I could hear Rickie's voice in my head.

"Bring an umbrella."

The hell with the umbrella. The hell with the rain.

The hell with Scotland. The hell with the entire bloody Island of Mist!

I get out of my car, and within a matter of seconds, I'm soaked, completely saturated, and my lovely Calvin Klein flats are covered with mud, squishing with every step, but I press on. Into the monsoon. I get to the gravesite, and I talk to my parents, engulfed in wetness, dripping with wetness, hatless, with all my freezing soaking clothes pressing against me, weighing a ton.

I was, of course, well-prepared for the weather, wearing a super-dumb hyper-absorbent cotton coat, a white cashmere sweater, and a cotton plaid skirt.

A blue-green MacDonald plaid.

When I finished saying whatever I said to my mom and my dad, I looked around. There was nothing but rain, falling in torrents, not a living soul, not even a distant pair of headlights. Then I saw a little thatched cottage at the far edge of the cemetery. Maybe there was a human being inside. Maybe, more importantly, there was a phone inside.

I started squishing my way across the graveyard, through the whipping rain.

Finally, I made it to the door of the cottage and knocked. The roof of the place looked like straw, like the worst of the three little pigs' houses, and I had very little confidence that it would be waterproof inside, but anything was better than standing out in the open, like Jane Eyre on the moors.

The door opened.

Naturally, it was the one person on the island, in the entire world, I didn't want to see.

The gravedigger.

Wearing his dark shades.

"You!" I said stupidly, wondering if I should turn around and offer myself to the storm again.

"My car's stuck in a ditch," I explained.

He said nothing.

Expressionless.

He wore jeans, a dark-blue flannel shirt, and a baseball cap that said "Sult Inn" across the front.

He shut the door in my face.

I was astonished.

I didn't know what to think, so I just stood there like an idiot staring at the wooden door.

Should I knock again?

Should I yell something?

Should I get angry?

Should I kick at the door in frustration?

Then the door reopened, and he handed me a soft yellow towel.

"Come in."

It was only two words, but it was the thickest brogue I'd ever heard.

I stepped inside and toweled off my face. For the first time, I realized that I was actually shivering, but it was warm and dry in his cozy living room. There was a pleasant stone fireplace, with a healthy fire, and a comfortable-looking couch, but I was much too wet to sit down. The weird kid from the tavern was sitting on a small wooden stool in front of a television screen. He was, similarly, wearing jeans, a flannel shirt, and a "Sult Inn" cap, but his shirt was red not blue.

He looked at me and smiled.

"Hi," I said pathetically.

He just looked at me and continued smiling. I wondered if he ever stopped smiling.

"His name is Jimmy," the gravedigger said.

I looked at the TV screen. It was paused on the face of Anne Elliot, actually the actress Sally Hawkins, wearing a pretty purplish bonnet. It was the ITV version of Jane Austen's *Persuasion*.

I knew it well.

Suddenly, I noticed that the gravedigger was gone, and I was all alone with the smiling boy and Sally Hawkins in her lovely bonnet. I stepped closer to the fireplace and glanced down at the wooden coffee table. There were three DVD's aside from the open *Persuasion* box: *Snow White*, *Sleeping Beauty*, and *Casablanca*.

The theme was obvious.

"Somebody likes love stories," I tried.

"Yes," he said.

He looked at me.

"So do you."

Was he reading my mind?

I nodded and looked at the kid for help.

"I could really use a compliment right now."

He didn't hesitate.

"Your step is music, and your voice is song."

I felt much better.

The gravedigger reentered the room holding a pile of clothes, looking like comfortable sweats. Probably Jimmy's.

"Use the bedroom at the end of the hall," he said. "It's Jimmy's room."

"Thank you."

I sloshed down the hall into the bedroom. The first thing I noticed was the picture of Matt. It was an action shot. Racing in his long-track, hoodless skinsuit. There were also pictures of Eric Heiden, Bonnie Blair, and Dan Jansen.

Eric Heiden, who's generally considered the greatest speedskater of all time, won five gold medals at the 1980 Winter Olympics in Lake Placid. He also set fifteen world records in his short career before becoming an orthopedic surgeon. Bonnie Blair, one of the great female athletes of all time, also won five gold medals spread over four Olympics, finishing at Lillehammer in 1994. Dan Jansen, the legendary sprinter, took several heartbreaking falls in the 1988 Olympics after his sister died of leukemia. Then, after more disappointment in 1992, he finally got his gold in the 500 meters at the 1994 Olympics. Over the course of his distinguished career, he set eight world records.

The reason I know all this stuff, of course, is because of Matt, because of our one-time relationship, but why did this strange kid in the Scottish Highlands have an interest in speedskating?

I had no idea.

I removed my clothes. Actually, I peeled them off and dropped them into a puddle on the floor. Then I toweled myself some more, before slipping into the soft warm sweats. Is there anything more comfortable in the world? The sweatshirt, obviously Jimmy's, had a picture of Snow White on the front.

I was fine with that.

I walked over to his little mirror. But this one was no "Magic Mirror." It reflected the sorry truth and nothing but the truth. I stared at the sorry creature in the glass. Hair matted like a wet rope, like a thatched roof, eyes red from the wind and the rain, skin cold and seemingly lifeless.

I hope it's not too vain to say, especially given the Snow White motif, but the Chocolate Princess is usually rather pretty.

My father once said I look like a young Deborah Kerr. A Scottish actress who was nominated for six Oscars, but who never won until they gave her an honorary statue for her "lifetime of work" in over fifty films. So I watched a few of her films: *The King and I*, *Black Narcissus*, and the famous tearjerker *An Affair to Remember*.

Like me, she had reddish-gold hair and blue-green eyes.

If anybody wants to compare me to the likes of

Deborah Kerr, I'm fine with that. Except for her romp in the sand with Burt Lancaster in *From Here to Eternity*, she generally played proper, graceful, quintessential Englishwomen. Even though she was a Scot.

Enough.

There was no Deborah Kerr staring back at me in the mirror. I realized that any attempt to rectify the horrific mess standing in front of me was pointless, so I left the room and returned to the two weirdos in the living room.

Jimmy took a look at me in his sweats:

She walks in beauty, like the night
Of cloudless climes and starry skies.

Well, there's nothing like a little Byron to make a girl feel better.

I looked at Jimmy, then the gravedigger.

"I'm sorry about last night. I'm truly ashamed of myself."

Jimmy responded, as if instinctively.

"Confessed faults are half-mended."

Ian smiled at Jimmy, then spoke to me.

"It's an old Scottish proverb. He knows thousands of them."

His brogue was soft and comforting.

"I was out of my mind last night," I tried to explain, as if it hadn't been perfectly obvious.

"Forget about it. We have. Right, Jimmy?"

Jimmy nodded, but I still felt the necessity to make excuses.

"My father died."

Which was probably a dumb thing to say to the gravedigger who'd buried him.

He nodded.

"Which you know, of course," I added.

"He's a hard man to lose."

I suddenly went soft again.

I felt ready to cry.

"Sit before the fire."

The gravedigger gestured to the couch, and I sat down. The warmth of the fire was comforting, but I was still upset.

"You might have a talk with Fr. Buchanan. He looks younger than he is, but he's always helpful."

Maybe I *should* talk to someone. I wasn't doing so well on my own.

"I'm Ian MacIan."

He reached toward me, and we shook hands.

"How about some hot cider? Or tea? Or coffee?

"Cider would be great."

He left the room again.

I noticed that the TV screen was now black. There was a "guest" in the house, and Jane Austen would have to wait. Lying near me on the couch was a worn-out copy of Scott's *Waverley*. His famous novel about the Jacobite uprising of 1745.

I looked at Jimmy who was looking at me.

"Somebody's been reading the classics," I said, wondering if we could have a normal conversation.

He nodded.

He nods a lot.

"Do you like it?" I tried.

"Yes."

Which wasn't much help, but he continued.

"Ian says it wavers too much."

I laughed.

My mother made sure that I read *all* the classics, and *Waverley* is the granddaddy of Scottish novels. But Ian was right. Edward Waverley, the main character, was always a bit too passive for my money. Hardly the affirmative type like Wentworth in Jane Austen's *Persuasion*."

"You prefer Wentworth?" I suggested.

"Yes."

"Who else?"

"Lochinvar."

I knew it by heart.

In Scott's great ballad, Lochinvar is a ridiculously courageous knight who turns up at the wedding of his true love, "the fair Ellen," then steals her away from her wimpy groom and her bloodthirsty kinsman, somehow escaping the relentless pursuit of the Netherby clan.

So daring in love, and so dauntless in war,
  Have ye e'er heard of gallant like young
  Lochinvar?

"Ian's like Lochinvar."

Well, I guess Mr. Gravedigger must be quite a guy! But it was very sweet to see how much Jimmy admired his older brother.

Assuming that he really *was* his older brother.

I changed the subject.

"I see you're a speedskating fan."

"Matthew Brooks is the best."

He seemed excited about the subject, adding:

"A gentleman too."

I wondered if his "tag on" was directed at me, but I doubted it. Jimmy, it seemed to me, was inherently guileless.

"Yes," I agreed, "he definitely is."

Then I shifted things a bit.

"What about you guys? Any sports?"

"Ian tosses the hammer."

"At the Highland Games?"

Now *I* was excited.

"Yes, first place at Cowal. Twice."

Wow!

I knew *all* about the Highland Games, attending them every summer with my parents in either upstate New York or Maine. Not to mention two trips to Grandfather Mountain in North Carolina. But the

Cowal Games were the *really* big games, taking place every August in Dunoon, Scotland, which I'd once attended when I was thirteen, completely overwhelmed with the pipes, the fiddles, the dancing, and of course, the caber toss, the stone put, and the hammer throw.

Ian reentered the room and handed me a red "Disneyland" mug, and I sipped at the hot cider.

"It's delicious!"

He seemed pleased.

I tried to keep things light.

"So I guess thatched rooves really work?"

He smiled.

"Aye, water reed is naturally waterproof, and every bundle is over fifteen-inches thick. Which is more than you need to know."

I smiled and looked at Jimmy.

"Any ghosts around here? I love ghost stories."

"Skye is the island of mist and ghosts."

I looked back at Ian.

"We've got our share at the cemetery, but most of them hang at the castles."

"Have you worked here long?"

"Yes, my whole life. I dig graves in the day and fiddle at night."

"Is it a good life?"

Which was probably a dumb question.

"Yes, it is."

"We're blessed, indeed!" Jimmy assured me.

I wondered if I'd ever heard the word "indeed"

used in normal conversation.

I took another sip from my Disney cup.

"Have you been to the States?"

"We went to Disneyland a few years ago," Ian explained.

"The Magic Kingdom!" Jimmy remembered.

I turned to Jimmy.

"Where else would you like to go?"

He didn't hesitate.

"New York City."

"What would you like to see?"

"The New Sult Inn."

Ian laughed.

Rickie told me this morning that there were plans to open a similar tavern in Manhattan.

"What else?"

"The Rabbie Burns statue."

"I know it well. I go there all the time. What else?"

"St. Anthony's Cemetery."

Which I suppose made some sense. I was now hanging with the "graveyard crowd," but I did wonder why *that* one in particular, being one I'd never heard of. Why not one of the more famous ones, like Woodlawn in the Bronx?

A clock chimed above the fireplace. It was eleven-thirty a.m., and I needed to pack for my flight.

But I didn't want to leave.

"It's so comfortable here. I'd love to stay as long as you'd have me, but I'm flying back tonight."

Ian understood.

"Of course."

He looked out the window.

"The rains letting up."

He looked at Jimmy.

"What's the number at the station?"

"02-5584."

Ian took out his phone and dialed.

"Music?"

It was Jimmy.

"Sure."

"Dion?"

"Sure."

"He's got four favorites," Ian explained, "fiddles, pipes, Anne Murray, and Dion."

I wasn't a huge Celine Dion fan, but I definitely liked her voice, and even though I'd never cared for that dumb *Titanic* movie, I loved the love song.

Ian got connected.

"Molly? It's Ian. Send Alistair over with his wrecker. I got a car stuck in a ditch. It's a Yank, so you can overcharge her."

I laughed.

Jimmy pressed a button on a little boombox, and something came out that definitely wasn't Celine Dion. It was lively, smooth, and it filled up the room. Whatever it was, I liked it. It made me want to dance. Even Jimmy was swaying lightly to the music. I looked at Ian.

"What kind of Dion is that?"

"Dion of 'Dion and the Belmonts.' It's called Doo-Wop. Late 50's, early 60's. We're even further behind than you thought."

"It's great."

It was a song called "I Wonder Why."

I made a mental note.

I wonder why I love you like I do,
Is it because I think you love me too?

When it was over, I said goodbye to Jimmy, and Ian handed me an old, black, hooded slicker. I put it on and stepped outside. It was still raining, still misty, but it didn't seem so intimidating.

Then, without a word, Ian went back inside the house, and I stood there alone, confused about everything. About absolutely everything. Off in the distance, I could see a green wrecker heading toward the cottage.

Then Ian was back.

He handed me a big green garbage bag.

"Your clothes," he explained.

I took the bag, but I was distracted, pensive.

"I'll walk you out," he said.

"I wish you wouldn't."

Which probably seemed odd, but he was expressionless as usual.

Maybe it's an appropriate time to try and describe

the Graveyard Knight. He was probably around my age, mid-twenties, tall, maybe 6'2", rugged, lean, and fit. Digging graves hadn't done him any harm. His hair, as I remembered from last night, was thick, slightly-unkempt, and dark brown, and his eyes, of course, were unknown and unseen behind his dark lenses. The best I can do is an "extrapolation" on the young Hugh Jackman.

But definitely a Scot, not an Aussie.

He was *very* easy to look at, as well as comfortable to be with.

"Thank you," I said.

It sounded kind of stupid.

Then I leaned into him, and I kissed him on the lips, like we were lovers. I lingered a bit, then I walked away.

He said nothing.

I headed to the wrecker.

What was wrong with me? I've never done anything like that in my life! I was definitely screwed-up and I knew it.

Maybe he was right.

Maybe I *did* need to talk to someone.

10. Kiss

Friday, October 30th

[Remembrance of Ian MacIan:]

I didn't want her to go.

Which should go without saying.

I wanted her to do it again.

I thought about the old Hitchcock movie. *To Catch a Thief.* With its famous Grace Kelly kiss. The "unexpected" kiss. That's what it was like, and I stood there just as dumbfounded as Cary Grant.

Besides, I knew it was all wrong.

Besides, I felt a little uneasy about what had happened earlier when she was in Jimmy's bedroom, soaked and changing her clothes.

We were waiting silently in the living room like a pair of idiots, when Jimmy said the kind of thing he'd never said before.

"Is she naked?"

I was stunned, but I didn't let on.

"You shouldn't be thinking about that."

I said it firmly, in my no-nonsense voice, but I also wondered if it was totally innocent. Maybe Jimmy had said it just like he might have said, "Does she have a hat on?" No one on the planet knew Jimmy better than me, but I wasn't sure.

"Were you?" he asked.

Which was the next shock.

I assumed it wasn't an accusation.

Once again, I assumed it was totally innocent, but it knocked me back a bit, even though I didn't show it.

"No, I wasn't, Jimmy. It's not polite."

Then I wondered if I *was* thinking about it, but I wasn't. I was off the hook. What I was really thinking about was how can I help this poor messed-up grief-stricken girl feel comfortable with the likes of me and Jimmy.

I was also thinking how lucky I was to have her here in my home.

How I needed to be kind.

How I needed to keep my distance.

11. St. Mary's

Friday, October 30th

I decided to stop at the church.

Despite my silly Snow White sweats.

St. Mary's is smallish and very attractive. An old-fashioned stone church with colorful stained-glass windows. Near the altar, a priest was sitting in the first pew reading a prayer book. When he heard me approaching, he turned around. He was small, old, and a bit wizened, with a shock of white hair and a welcoming smile.

"I'm looking for Fr. Buchanan."

"That would be me, lassie."

He certainly wasn't the young priest I was expecting.

His brogue was almost as thick as Ian's.

"I believe you knew my father, Angus Kinnell?"

"Aye. A finer man than any."

I was touched by his kindness.

"Could we talk about it? I'm a bit of a mess right

now."

"Of course."

A few minutes later, I was sitting in an upright chair in a small reception room. The room was flat white, comfortable, and uncluttered. On the wall behind the old priest was the room's only decoration: a four-foot wooden crucifix. As I stumbled through my "problems," he did his best to help.

"Time doesn't 'heal' things, Polly. Only the grace of God."

It wasn't much help, and he knew it, so he pressed on.

"Believe me, I know. At my age, I've lost everyone. Brothers, sisters, friends, nieces, and nephews. Just Monday, I was burying one of my nephews in Aberdeen, which is why I wasn't at your father's funeral."

I understood.

"Loss is suffering," he explained, "and nothing some old priest can say will make it better. You need to offer it up, in sacrifice, and be grateful that your father was such a marvelous man, now with the angels, now with your lovely mother, who was an angel herself."

I thought it over. I believed he was right, so I changed the subject.

"Ian MacIan implied you were a young priest."

He smiled.

"Aye, Ian likes his laugh, his bit of mischief. But it *is* true that I look younger than I am."

"Can I ask?"

"A hundred plus two."

I was guessing eighty or so.

"You don't look a day over seventy."

He smiled again.

"Good genes and exercise."

I laughed.

Then it was his turn to change the subject.

"Tell me about your work, Polly. I've never regretted the priesthood until the day your father told me his daughter made her living as a chocolate taster."

"Well, it's really quite simple. Several different companies 'fly me in' twice a year to evaluate their products. The chemical combinations in chocolate can create over 400 distinct flavors, so every piece of chocolate is different, and what the companies want me to do is evaluate their current products against their own standards. Godiva wants their chocolate to taste like Godiva chocolate."

"Is there much pressure?"

"Not really. To be honest, it's pretty easy since all chocolate chefs are perfectionists. All I have to do is report the good news. With maybe a suggestion or two."

He was definitely intrigued.

"It's sounding a lot like whiskey tasting, which I've done a bit of myself over the years."

"It's very similar. We even use a lot of the same terms they use for whiskey and wine tasting. But I have to evaluate other things as well, like appearance, the 'snap' of the chocolate, the texture, and the aftertaste."

"Do you have a specialty?"

"My father trained me to be receptive to everything, but I actually prefer milk chocolate the best. Connoisseurs, of course, prefer dark chocolate with its higher cocoa content and minimal sugar. But my tastes are more pedestrian. More bourgeoisie."

He laughed, then he looked at me slyly.

"What's your favorite?"

"My dad's milk chocolate, of course!"

It was a diplomatic answer, as well as a true one, but the old priest wanted more.

"What else?"

"Can you keep a secret?"

"I've been keeping secrets for a hundred years."

"I can never resist Callebaut gourmet from Belgium. Having said that, I'm perfectly willing to buy a yummy Hershey bar in any supermarket on the planet."

The church bells tolled.

"It's time for my mid-days. Where I'll certainly express my gratitude for the pleasures of chocolate. And for meeting Miss Polly Kinnell."

He stood up.

I did as well.

I didn't want him to leave.

"What's the story with the gravedigger?"

"It's a long story, my dear."

"Tell me a bit."

"Ian's a very special young man. Far more than meets the eye. A lad who's got the 'gift' as well."

Which was terribly vague.

Maybe intentionally.

"Who," he added, "takes very good care of his cousin, young Jimmy. Whom he homeschools at the cottage."

I was amazed.

"He does?" I said stupidly.

"He most certainly does."

I was homeschooled by my mother, and I knew everything that it involved. Later, when I asked her why she did it, she looked at me oddly, as if I'd learned nothing.

"Because I didn't want anyone else doing it."

Which made perfect sense.

Then she added.

"Besides, who else would teach you Scottish history?"

I had no answer for that.

The bells chimed again.

"Time to go," he said.

"Time for me to fly back to New York."

"God will bless you, bonnie Polly. Though you may not notice at first."

He blessed me, and left, and I still had a million more questions that would have to go unanswered.

I wished I could take him with me.

12. Tastings

November 10th–20th

The Chocolate Queen visits her dominions.

Most of mid-November, I was on the road.

Starting in Ghirardelli Square. Even though their production was moved to San Leandro back in 1967, I still met with the execs and the chefs at their old headquarters on the Square, right where Domingo Ghirardelli first set up shop in 1895. Not far from the Golden Gate, Alcatraz, and Fisherman's Wharf.

As I remember, I told them something like this:

The touch of malt is exactly right. As is the tart in the aftertaste. Similarly, the scent of the chocolate is as rich as it should be, with a whisper of honey. The texture's also perfect, but I'm not sure that the snap's just right. It should be louder. It might be remedied by increasing the percentage of the cocoa, especially that new Brazilian blend. But, all in all, the chocolate is exquisite, as always, and exquisitely your own.

Something like that.

With a full report to be submitted later.

Since the Ghirardelli boys are always a fun group, I surprised them with (of all things) a little poem about the history of chocolate. It's a sonnet by some unknown poet whom I've never heard of.

I read it aloud.

Unsurprisingly, it's called "Chocolate":

Why did Montezuma give his guest,
Hernán Cortés, that rather bitter "tea"
his Aztec farmers had carefully pressed
from the tropical seeds of the cacao tree?
And why did the Dominican friars bring
it back to Spain, from where, by chance,
the young María, engaged to the Bourbon King,
would introduce the "sweetened" drink to
  France?
And why, from London, did Mr. Fry present
to the waiting world the "chocolate bar," well
  worth
its weight in gold, and why did Nestlé invent
"milk" chocolate, the greatest thing on earth?
To please, of course, my love, watching her
  DVR,
emparadised, eating her chocolate bar.

To which I added my own stupid couplet:

*Who cried out, "Love, I crave more sweets in
   my belly,
Bring me that giant box of Ghirardelli!"*

It was a bit hit.

Next stop: Brussels.

Not for the insignificant stuff like the Royal Palace, NATO, or the European Union, but for the headquarters of Godiva Chocolate, founded by Joseph Draps in 1926, located on the famous Grand-Place, where Draps' secret recipe has been carefully guarded for nearly a century.

Grand-Place has been called the most beautiful town square in the world, and its old baroque guildhalls are certainly stunning, especially Hôtel de Ville, Maison du Roi, and Le Pigeon, where Victor Hugo once lived.

But as for me, give me the little Godiva shop in the Royal Gallery of St. Hubert anytime. Any day of the week.

Which is where we always met.

In a back room.

As always, I cleared my palate with water and some apple slices, then luxuriated in Godiva chocolates, which, excepting my father's chocolates, were my mother's favorite.

He once told me that when he first saw my mother

she was eating a Godiva Classic on a small bench in front of the Queen Mother Library at the University of Aberdeen, where he instantly fell in love with Bonnie Jean MacDonald.

She was studying European history at Aberdeen, with an emphasis on the Vikings, the Celts, and the Highlanders. With no interest, at the moment, in the male of the species. Until one of them walked up and said:

'What if I told you there was a better chocolate than Godiva?"

"I'd say you were a liar."

"What if I convinced you? Would you let me take you to dinner?"

"I'd do better than that, I'd marry you."

Which she did.

My mother's version of the story was pretty much the same. He always claimed that he had no idea "what I was doing," but he felt emboldened by the sight of the chocolate on her lips.

She said that he was shaking in his boots, and they often laughed about it.

Now they're gone.

Both of them.

But I mustn't "drift off" into sorrows, even though it's a lovely little love story within this much longer love story, which I hope is acceptable.

Anyway, back to Brussels.

Where I told the suits and the chefs something like

this:

> *The vanilla tang is right on the money.*
> *Excellent! And the texture's as creamy as it*
> *should be. Marvelously so. But the aftertaste*
> *seems a little bit flatter than in the past,*
> *especially with the milk chocolate. But the snap*
> *is still crisp, with a nice loud "pop," and the*
> *sheen is perfect. You always live up to the chefs*
> *of Godiva past.*

The full report was along the same lines.
Mostly praise, with a few nitpicks.
Yes, I *do* have the greatest job in the world.
But it's also the easiest.
How do you *really* test chocolate? It's as simple as
the old saying:

> *Chocolate should make you smile.*

Which it certainly did in Brussels.
Then I recited the chocolate poem with a new and
rather dreadful appendage:

> *My love was salivating, flush with saliva,*
> *Yelling out, "Sweetheart, bring more Godiva."*

When they finished laughing, I flew back across
the ocean and landed in Hersheyland.

Yeah, the stuff might be cheap, but it's still perfectly delicious, as every grammar school kid in the world can testify.

Milton Hershey was an extraordinary visionary. A chocolatier who built a chocolate empire, but who was also a philanthropist who created an amazing community of chocolate workers. With schools and homes and playgrounds and excellent wages. He also financed serious scientific research into the cocoa bean, establishing an experimental cocoa tree farm down in Belize.

These days, Hersheyland is also an amusement park where kids can ride roller coasters, swim in the water park, and learn about the history and "making" of chocolate.

I have to admit, I love the place. I love its history. I love its Hershey chefs. Many of whom, I've known since I was as a child.

So what did I tell them?

More of the same kind of stuff:

As always, you've got the best aftertaste in the business! The texture's appropriately smooth, even velvety. I did notice a slight bloom on the dark chocolate, but the snap was just right, and the flavors were fresh and pleasant. In my opinion, it tastes exactly like a classic Hershey bar should taste.

Then I read them the sonnet with yet another ridiculous appendage:

> *I looked at my sweet love and thought: "Were she*
> *Still hungry, I'd bring her a ton of Hershey.*

Yeah, I know! The rhyme's embarrassing, but let's see *you* come up with a better rhyme for "Hershey."

Or "Godiva," for that matter.

Anyway, they loved it.

Later that night, I was back on a jet heading home to New York City. I was finishing up *Persuasion*. I'd read the novel with my mother years ago, but now the terrible romantic agonies of Miss Anne Elliot, whom a lot of people believe was Austen herself, seemed to resonate much deeper in my own life.

When I finished the book, I returned to the penultimate chapter, where Anne is about to read the crucial letter, of which Jane Austen describes: "On the contents of that letter depended all which this world could do for her!"

Containing the crucial line.

The most crucial line in Anne's life.

The most crucial line in *anyone's* life.

Six simple words:

> *I have loved none but you.*

I put the book away.

I've done my best to describe my November chocolate travels as nothing but fun. Nothing but pleasure. But there were also difficult times when I was alone. Slowly, *very* slowly, I was learning to appreciate and enjoy my life again. To deal with the devastating loss of my father. To try and forget all the trouble I'd caused in Scotland.

But for some reason, I could never forget the gravedigger.

Just as Anne Elliot could never forget Wentworth.

There was even a letter.

Moving in the opposite direction.

A carefully worded, handwritten letter from the Chocolate Princess to the Graveyard Knight, apologizing once again, thanking him for his kindness, wishing him and Jimmy "all the best," but never mentioning the kiss in the rain and never attempting to describe the inexplicable attractions I was still feeling.

Which were perfectly ridiculous.

I didn't even know the guy, and he lived three thousand miles away.

In a cemetery!

In response, there was nothing.

No text, no email, no letter.

Nothing.

Which bothered me more than it should have. Which felt like one more "loss." One more "lack" that I'd have to learn to live with.

On the trips to Frisco, then Belgium, then Hershey, I never told the chefs and the suits about the "other" sonnet that that same unknown poet had written about chocolate. It was much too stupid, too sad, too ridiculous, too unreadable.

"Death by Chocolate":

Hey, sweetheart, I just wanted you to know
there'll be no razors, pills, or smacked-up cars
cause ever since you left me three weeks ago,
I've been killing myself with chocolate bars.
The problem is I'm liking it a lot:
the highs are great, so much better than drink,
and I feel fantastic. I guess that I forgot
this stuff is more nutritious than people think.
My friends, of course, believe I've lost my mind,
and I can understand why they're uptight,
they feel my diet's a little bit confined,
but I'm convinced that things'll be all right.
As for your message, sorry, I've got some doubt,
I'm not so sure I want to "work things out."

Yeah, the guy who wrote this weirdo poem must have been a basketcase. Maybe that's why nobody's ever heard of him. But let's face it, who hasn't taken a few beatings of the heart and considered chocolacide?

13. Kinnell's Manhattan

Monday, December 14th

I was wearing a ridiculous red elf's hat, and, once again, I was staring at Rickie's twelve brats, but they seemed a lot less intimidating on my own turf.

Especially since I'd already drugged them.

With you-know-what.

"Let it melt in your mouth."

Which they did, as per my instructions.

"It melts at body temperature," I added pointlessly.

To be honest, they were rather cute when they were stoned.

"When it's all gone, when the chocolate's sadly melted away, enjoy the lovely aftertaste, which can linger for hours."

Smarty-pants blondie had her own opinion.

"I like the taste better than the aftertaste."

It was hard to argue.

"Me too," I agreed.

Then blondie, as the apparent alpha of the group,

turned around and looked at Rickie.

"We'd like more."

She clearly spoke for the group, and the mob was behind her.

Rickie shrugged helplessly.

After all, it was Christmas.

Eleven days away.

As always, Aunt Katie had Kinnell's Manhattan looking festive and lovely, with Christmas music playing softly over the speakers.

"All right," Rickie conceded, "but that's it. I promised your parents we'd do less than four ounces each."

The kids didn't care about ounces.

The little heads swung back to me.

Two dozen eager eyes, high on sugar, craving more.

"Excellent," I said, as I began placing another milk chocolate square on each of the little white napkins sitting in front of my twelve little druggies.

In my opium den.

At the moment, the store was empty except for Rickie and the kids and Aunt Katie, who was back in the office. I knew she was worried about something, and I had my suspicions.

I looked at Rickie.

"I'll be back in a few minutes. If any *real* customers come in, call me."

Back in her cluttered office, my aunt, also wearing

a red elf's hat, sat pensively at her desk.

"What's the matter, Aunt Katie?"

"Oh, I'm fine, dearie," she lied. "Don't you worry about a thing."

I pulled a chair over, sat down in front of her, and took her hands in mine.

Looking into her eyes.

"Tell me what's wrong."

"I don't want to spoil Christmas."

"Tell me."

"We're not doing too well."

I waited for the rest.

"I'm sure we'll have another wonderful Christmas, but we've had a gradual falling off ever since your father left for Scotland. It was never dramatic, but it's added up over the past four years, and we're in trouble, my dear."

Just as I'd suspected.

"I guess we need another Scotsman," she kidded. "No one charmed the customers like your father."

"How much do we need?"

I took out my checkbook.

"I'm not taking any of your money, Polly."

I looked at her intently.

"Look, Aunt Katie, we're co-owners. Right? And I don't do much around here, so let me do this. Besides, we're losing the store in Scotland, and this is all I have left of my father's legacy, and I don't want it to go under. Besides, I make plenty of money. You know that."

She didn't argue.

"Tell me how much you need, and don't lie."

"It's a lot, Polly."

"Tell me."

"Thirty-five thousand would break us even. It would also allow me to keep the part-time help over Christmas."

I scribbled out a check and handed it to my aunt.

"I can't tell you," I explained, "how good this makes me feel. Do you understand that?"

"Yes."

"Will you tell me when you need more?"

"Yes."

"Promise?"

"Yes."

"It's what my dad would have wanted."

She knew it was true.

Then a man's voice called out from the front of the store.

"How about some service out here?"

I recognized his voice, so did my aunt.

She smiled.

"Why don't you take care of this one?"

I stood up, kissed my aunt on the cheek, and went out to the front.

Matt was standing at the counter. He was wearing an open black trench, probably a Burberry, with a blue-tinted dress shirt and a sharp blue blazer. As always, he looked remarkably handsome.

I looked across the counter and smiled.

"Are you stalking me?"

"Maybe I am. It's a lovely idea."

Rickie was bundling up the brats, doing her best to eavesdrop.

"What can I get you?" I asked my customer.

"How about some chocolate?"

"For your girlfriend?"

"I don't have a girlfriend, and if I *had* the one I want, chocolate would be the last thing she'd need."

We now had an audience.

Rickie had rounded up her charges near the front door, and all of them were watching closely. It seems my failed love life was oddly fascinating to chocolate-high five-year-olds.

When I didn't respond, Matt continued.

"I once had a girlfriend who told me that the best thing in the world is Kinnell's milk chocolate squares."

"Was she right?"

"She's always right."

I could see that Rickie liked that one.

Matt pointed to the squares under the glass counter.

"I'll take two pounds."

I got out a little white box and started weighing the squares. I could sense that some of the little eavesdroppers were getting antsy.

"Why not come to Lake Placid this weekend?"

Matt said. "It's the US championships."

Rickie, not wanting to lose her flock, explained what was happening.

In a teacherly fashion.

"That's speedskating, students. Very fast ice skating. The big guy who once dumped Miss Polly is an Olympic champion."

Which re-focused their attention.

I shrugged, non-committal.

"No strings attached, Polly."

Matt looked over at the teacher and tried to strengthen his hand.

"Bring Rickie along."

I put the white box in a white Kinnell's bag and handed it over to Matt.

"It's been paid for," I said. I certainly wasn't about to take his money.

"Should I bother to argue?"

I shook my head, and he took the bag and turned around to Rickie.

"By the way, Rickie, you're looking great, but I suspect you've been working too hard. Why not take a break this weekend?"

He held up two tickets.

"As someone once said, 'It's been paid for.'"

Then he turned around and placed them on the counter.

Right in front of me.

"Will you think about it?"

Rickie yelled out from the entrance, from the midst of her well-behaved dozen.

"You bet she will!"

I laughed. What else could I do.

"All right, I'll *think* about it."

Matt got serious.

Very serious.

"I love you, Polly Kinnell, and if I had any guts, I'd lean over this counter and kiss you on the mouth."

The kids loved it. Maybe they'd never seen a "live" profession of love before. Just on television.

The little redhead boy called out.

"Go ahead! Kiss her!"

The other brats joined in.

"Do it! Do it!"

But Matt looked at the kids, shrugged, and walked to the door. Then he nodded to Rickie and was gone.

The brats were clearly disappointed, and I was afraid they might boo, but Rickie intervened.

"Love is tough, kids. We'll discuss this in class. Now we need to thank Miss Kinnell for all the chocolate.

Which they all did. Excessively.

When Rickie and her brood were finally gone, another customer came in the store, and my aunt helped her out. As for me, I just stood there, behind the counter, totally confused.

Someone was singing, "I'll Be Home for Christmas."

It wasn't the Bing version, but it was lovely.
And sad.

I'll be home for Christmas
If only in my dreams.

I went back to the office and sat down. There was a framed picture of my father on the desk. He was dressed in a MacDonald blue-green plaid kilt. Smiling. Maybe in Scotland. Maybe on Skye. I hadn't cried since October 30th in the cottage with Ian and Jimmy.

My father won't "be home" for Christmas.
This year or any year.
I made up my mind not to cry.
It didn't work.

14. Córdoba's

Monday, December 14th

I was still wearing my silly elf's hat.

Why not?

Rickie and I were knocking off fajitas and strawberry margaritas, and I was trying to be encouraging.

"He'll come through. Don't worry about it."

She was worrying about her little school's primary donor, the anonymous one.

"If he doesn't come through, I'll never be able to expand next year."

"He'll come through," I repeated, "and if he doesn't, I'll help you out."

"You already have, but I need a lot more."

She pulled out an opened envelope.

"His last letter had the same postmark."

"Vermont?"

"Yeah."

"You know anybody up there?" I wondered.

"No. But Matt competes there sometimes."

I shrugged.

"He competes everywhere."

"Then who could it be?"

"Somebody who likes kids and likes what you're doing for them. Especially for the kids whose families can't afford it."

"I hope so."

I reached over, grabbed one of her jalapeños, and took a bite.

"Wow, that's brutal!"

A neutron bomb was imploding in my throat.

"You shouldn't be eating those things," she said.

"Yeah, you're right."

"Is somebody down in the dumps?"

There was that word again.

"Yeah, maybe too many margaritas have got me thinking about my dad again. Besides, I'm very confused about Matty."

"Then unconfuse yourself. Go to Lake Placid and see if there's anything there. See if you have an interest in a handsome, kind, famous, perfect guy who worships the ground you walk on. It sounds *really* confusing."

I laughed.

"Well, if I *really* wanted to figure things out, I'd have to go alone."

"Not a chance, sister! I'm heading north!"

I took another bite of the little chili pepper. If they weren't so painful, they'd be delicious.

Then I heard my name.

"Polly Kinnell?"

I turned around and saw Jack Cooper standing over the table. Jack was my GP in Scotch Plains. He'd taken over his dad's practice when his father died. But Jack was more than just our family doctor, he was a close friend of the family. A smart and caring guy in his mid-thirties, now wearing a nice blue suit, probably Brooks Brothers.

"Jack! It's great to see you!

I introduced him to Rickie.

"This is my best friend Rickie Moreno."

Then I explained to Rickie.

"And this is Dr. Jack Cooper, my 'Jersey' doctor."

"From the car crash?" she wondered.

"Yes, that's right," Jack said.

The semester before I met Rickie at Columbia, I was in a serious accident on the Garden State Parkway. Some drunk sideswiped my car near Exit 132, and I slammed into an overpass. I was "blacked" for several days, but when I woke up in Mountainside Hospital, my father, my mother, and Jack Cooper were standing at the edge of my bed. Somehow, except for the blackout, I came through the whole mess without any lingering damage.

I've always felt blessed in some weird kind of way. Grateful to be alive. Rickie, of course, knew the entire story, not that I ever remembered that much.

Obviously, Rickie remembered Jack's name.

They stared at each other.

Did I mention that Jack's a looker? A boy-next-door type, trim, fit, with soft blue eyes.

Rickie was wearing a bright red Christmas sweater, which might have looked ridiculous, but it actually enhanced her natural exoticism.

Her black eyes.

Her thick black hair.

They shook hands, and I thought I sensed some sparks.

I hated to interrupt, but I did anyway.

"I got your nice card when my dad died."

"He was a great man, Polly. I wish I could have gone to Scotland and said farewell."

Rickie butted in.

"You would have enjoyed yourself. Polly got drunk and made a perfect fool of herself."

Jack laughed, and I changed the subject.

"Why don't you sit down?"

"Yeah," Rickie agreed, "we haven't eaten with a good-looking man in months."

He laughed again, and I tried to explain.

"She's from the Bronx."

Now it was Jack's turn.

"There's nothing lovelier than a pretty woman with a Bronx accent."

Which finally shut her up.

Then he turned back to me.

"I can't stay, Polly. I'm in the city for a medical

conference at Columbia, and I've got to get going."

He nodded over at the front door where a woman and two men, surely fellow doctors, were waiting.

"Don't work too hard, Jack," I said, which sounded rather stupid.

"You take care, Polly."

Then he turned to Rickie.

"It was great meeting you."

She nodded weakly, as Jack turned around and left.

I grabbed another jalapeño.

Rickie slapped playfully at my hand.

"No more of those for you!"

"OK, last one. I had no idea these things were so delicious."

Then I torched my mouth with another bite and drowned the agony with delicious margarita.

Staring at Rickie, mischievously.

"I think he likes you."

"Fine, then set me up."

"I will, but he's a workaholic like you. You'll never see each other."

"Fine, just set me up."

"I will."

She looked at me suspiciously.

"Why aren't *you* interested?"

"Jack's like family. Like a cousin."

"Some people marry their cousins."

I laughed.

She wasn't finished.

"You know what I think?"

"I'm sure I'm going to know real soon."

"I think you've got that gravedigger on your brain."

"I've got *nothing* on my brain right now," I assured her, "and I like it that way!"

I finished off my chili with more margarita.

"Yum!" I said.

"You're an idiot," she said.

I couldn't disagree.

15. Apartment

Tuesday, December 15th

I woke up.

Something was wrong.

My life had changed.

There was no pain. There was no burn. There was no unusual taste in my mouth.

But something was wrong.

It was still dark outside, so I checked the clock. It was four in the morning.

4:13.

I got out of bed, walked past Rickie's room, into the kitchen. I opened the refrigerator and looked at the stuff inside. Rickie's mostly-junky stuff, and my mostly-healthy stuff, with lots in between. I took out some green grapes and popped one in my mouth.

It tasted horrible.

Flat. Lifeless.

It's hard to describe.

I put the grapes back, went to the bathroom, and

stared at the idiot in the mirror.

"What have you done to yourself?"

To be certain, I rinsed out my mouth with water. As I put the cup back, I knocked Rickie's hairdryer off the wall and it crashed to the floor.

It was pretty loud, but I couldn't undo it.

I took the toothpaste tube. Crest. Then I squeezed a bit onto my forefinger and put it into my mouth.

There was no doubt.

Rickie entered the little room behind me. Groggy, concerned.

"What's going on?"

I turned around.

"I can't taste anything."

16. Medical Center

Tuesday, December 15th

"What's the good news?"

I was being sarcastic with myself.

It was seven hours after the toothpaste, and I was sitting in an examining room with Dr. Edward Prescott, an ENT specialist at New York-Presbyterian. He was staring at my test results.

He looked at me directly.

He was an older white-haired man, a big shot in his field. He didn't mince words, but he still did his best to be upbeat.

"You might get better."

"Might?" I said, attempting to ward off the panic, the desperation.

Then there was a sudden knock on the door, and Jack Cooper came into the room. Early this morning, I'd called him at the Marriott on Broadway where he was staying during his medical conference. He recommended Prescott, then he made a few calls.

The older doctor looked over, glad to see him.

"Hey, Jack."

"Hey, Ed. How's she doing?"

"She's burned her tongue pretty bad."

He looked at me.

"You've damaged your taste buds, and they're not going to work very well for a while."

"How long?"

"It's impossible to say. I wish I could."

I asked the deadly question.

"Could it be permanent?"

"I doubt it. There'll be some kind of regeneration, but I don't know if you'll ever get back to normal."

I didn't say a word. Normal for me wasn't like normal for everyone else.

"I'll prescribe some mouthwash for the burn, and I'll see you again in three weeks."

"Three weeks!"

He looked at me in a fatherly kind of way.

"I'm sorry, Ms. Kinnell, but this'll take some time. You'll need to be patient."

I didn't feel patient.

"Do you know what I do for a living?"

He seemed confused.

"I thought you said you owned a chocolate shop?"

"I do, but it's not my main job. I'm a taster. For several chocolate firms. It's my living."

"I'm very sorry," he repeated. "Hopefully things'll work out."

"I have people depending on me," I said to no one
in particular.

Having done his best, the specialist left the room,
and Jack sat down in the chair next to me.

"I wish I could say something comforting."

"I know, Jack," I said. "Thanks for coming.

Not knowing what else to say.

17. Central Park

Wednesday, December 15th

I was sitting on a bench in Central Park facing the Rabbie Burns statue at the south end of Literary Walk. It was my favorite place in the park.

It was a brisk but pleasant December afternoon.

I hope you're not getting tired of all my recent problems and sorrows. Until my dad died, I'd never spent much time feeling sorry for myself. My mother's death four years ago was terribly difficult, but I still had my dad to help me through. Now I had no one. Except for Rickie, who was doing her best. It also didn't help that Matt had suddenly popped back into my life, confusing things, confusing everything.

Not to mention my totally illogical feelings for some distant Scotsman named Ian MacIan.

Now, I didn't even have a job.

Or my one true talent.

As mentioned, my condition was hard to describe. Yes, I could still taste things, but everything seemed flat. Leveled out. My ability to make fine distinctions was gone. Everything was toneless. Strawberry ice cream still tasted good and sweet, but it tasted like every other strawberry ice cream. Haagen-Dazs tasted like Breyers, and vice versa. I'd lost my powers of discernment, something that I'd carefully developed, with my father's help, ever since I was a little girl, which I'd stupidly destroyed two nights ago with a few killer jalapeños.

I'd spent my entire adult life eating carefully. Protecting my palate. Protecting my one-and-only uniqueness.

Now it was gone.

A few weeks ago, I found another poem on the web by that same hapless poet who'd written the two chocolate sonnets. The new one was about a guy who's pathetically clinging to a lost love.

It's called "Aftertaste."

Something I know a lot about:

> *He never even noticed anymore*
> *the "finish" of the wine, the tang of the salt,*
> *the sweetness of the sugared petit four,*
> *the curry, the chili, or the bitters in his malt.*
> *Not that he minded when flavors stayed behind*
> *and lingered, subtly, persistently, instead*
> *of fading away. Of course, he didn't mind;*
> *it was the essence of the life he led:*
> *ever since you said good-bye and shut*

> *the door, ten years ago, March twenty-two,*
> *his whole existence has been nothing but*
> *the ineradicable residue,*
> *the unrelenting flavored déjà vu,*
> *the sweet stupendous aftertaste of you.*

Yeah, the guy's desperation is both pitiful and embarrassing, but I envy the fact that he still maintains the specificity of his lover's aftertaste.

Not to mention the fact that, at one time, he actually *had* the love he still wanted to love.

Back here in the real world, I'm stuck with negligible aftertaste and no real future. Five years ago, when I was first hired at Ghirardelli's, I stopped taking a salary at the shop on Fifth Avenue. After all, I only worked there about fifteen hours a week, and I was often away on tasting trips. Besides, I was soon making money hand over fist, and I had the sense that, financially, Aunt Katie and the store were treading water.

Now I've got *no* salary, *no* job, *no* parents, and *no* boyfriend.

Thank goodness for Rickie.

So here I am, sitting on my favorite "thinking" bench, and *not* feeling, as Rickie would say, down in the dumps. At least not *too* far down in the dumps. It was a lovely day, nine days till Christmas, and I knew that I was still more fortunate than so many other people in this world.

If not most.

I looked up and saw Rickie, bundled in her navy pea coat and carrying a newspaper under her arm, coming down the Literary Walk toward me.

Stopping in front of me.

"I figured I'd find you here."

She sat down and immediately put her arm around me. Which was indescribably comforting.

"Are you moping?" she wondered.

"Not as much as I could be."

She laughed, then gave me some unsolicited advice.

"Just try to buy some time, Polly. Tell those chocolate people that you're sick. Which is true. Tell them that you need a break for a few months. Maybe you'll be OK by then."

"Maybe."

"If not, maybe you can put in more hours at the store?"

I nodded.

"That wouldn't be so bad, right? Aunt Katie's a sweetheart."

"Yes, but the store's in trouble, Rickie. Katie's barely making enough to pay herself and the part-time help."

She didn't know.

So we sat there and looked up at the Scottish poet.

Naturally, I love the Burns statue, but I have to admit it's a bit overdramatic. He's sitting up there, on top of a tree stump, holding a quill pen, and looking upward into the heavens.

For inspiration.

He's bronze, on a pedestal, and larger than life.

"What's with the scroll at his feet?" Rickie asked.

"It's part of one of his poems," I explained. "To Mary in Heaven."

She was curious.

"Give me a taste."

She knew that my mom had me memorize all of his best poems when I was a kid.

Which I much enjoyed.

My Mary! Dear departed shade!
Where is thy place of blissful rest?
See'st thou thy lover lowly laid?
Hear'st thou the groans that rend his breast?

"I thought the guy was a serial philanderer?"

"He was, but when he was still young, he met Mary Campbell."

"Who's that?"

"A servant girl who worked for the Montgomerys of Coilsfield. They met on the banks of the Ayr, fell in love, and made some kind of 'lover's pact' involving two Bibles. They were planning to run off to the Caribbean. To Jamaica. Then, after they'd only known each other a month, Mary left for the Western Highlands to make final arrangements to emigrate, but she ended up nursing her brother, who had typhus. Tragically, she contracted the disease as well, dying five months after she'd left Burns. Dying at the age of twenty-three. When Burns was twenty-seven, after they'd only spent a month together."

"Whoa!"

"Yeah, it busted him up pretty bad."

"Tell me about Mary."

"She was tall, fair-haired, fair-complected, and blue-eyed. A Highland prototype. By all accounts, she was as kindly as she was lovely. Burns called her his 'Highland lassie,' and he wrote that she was "a warm-hearted charming young creature as ever blessed a man with generous love.'"

"Double-whoa!"

"Yeah, he wrote at least three poems about her. Here's another taste."

> *'Till the mortal stroke shall lay me low,*
> *I'm thine, my Highland lassie, O.*

"How do you remember all this stuff?"

"How could I forget?"

She thought it over. I certainly wouldn't call Rickie one of the great sentimentalists, but she was definitely affected.

"You Scots are a mushy crowd."

"Like Italians aren't."

She shrugged.

We went back to silence for a while. Then she opened her newspaper and changed the subject.

"Look what I spotted, Polly. Guess who's coming to the Roxie?"

I had no idea.

She held up the advertisement.

There was a picture of Dion.

Dion DiMucci.

"Isn't that the old rock stuff I hear you playing in your room?"

"Yeah. He's a favorite of Jimmy's."

"Let's go. A night at the Roxie would do you good. Me too. We haven't been to a concert in months.

"Sure," I decided. "Why not?"

Rickie was pleased.

But she could never stay silent for long.

"You know what I think?"

"What do you think, Rickie Moreno?"

"I think you should give Matt another chance."

Maybe she was right.

"Maybe I will."

18. Lake Placid

Friday, December 18th

"I can't stand it!"

She was about to explode.

With anticipation.

Bundled up, wearing our "USA" wool caps, we were standing in the tenth row of the grandstands over Sheffield Oval in Lake Placid. The same long-track where Eric Heiden won his five gold medals in the 1980 Olympics.

Matt was standing on the inner lane of the track. He was dressed in his classic, navy, aerodynamic "body suit" with an American flag on his left shoulder. At 6'3", he stood high on his 17-inch blades.

He looked fantastic.

In the outside lane was Josh Friedland, a young hot-shot sprinter from Wisconsin.

It was the final pairing of the US 500 meters.

"Don't worry, Rickie," I assured her, "Matt always wins the 500."

She wasn't so sure.

"How can you be so calm?"

"I know him better than anyone else."

The skaters took their positions.

Rickie had locked our arms, and she was literally jumping up and down with nervous agitation. I was also a bit nervous, but I'd seen Matt race countless times before, and I was used to the stress.

The skaters dug in.

They froze.

The gun went off.

Despite his size, Matt was notoriously quick off the mark. The two of them blitzed forward, assaulting the ice, hitting nearly forty miles an hour.

It was over, as they say, in the blink of an eye.

About 35 seconds.

The crowd went nuts.

Matt had crushed the kid, and now it was simply a question of whether he'd set any new records.

Down on the ice, Matt skated over to the base of the grandstands, pulled back his hood, and waved.

To me.

"Wave you idiot!"

I did as I was told.

Then Matt turned around and looked at the scoreboard. So did everyone else.

"33.97."

It was two seconds off his world record, but it was still the second-best time ever recorded in the 500. The crowd applauded loudly, and Matt waved his thanks.

I was proud of him, as always.

"He's magnificent," Rickie decided. "I wish he had the hots for me!"

I laughed.

Then Matt skated over to the first row to talk to someone in the stands.

It was Jimmy!

I was astonished.

I could see his lovely smile from twelve rows back.

I looked at Rickie.

"How about some hot chocolate?"

"Sure."

"I'll be right back."

Gradually, I made my way down to the front row. Matt had already skated off, but Jimmy was still beaming.

Then he saw me coming.

"Bonny Miss Polly!"

"Hey, Jimmy. What are you doing here?"

"Matthew Brooks is the best."

"Yes, he is."

"A gentleman too."

"Yes, he is."

Ian popped up. He was wearing a lined black leather jacket, a Sult Inn baseball cap, and his ubiquitous shades. He smiled at me, then handed a cup to Jimmy.

"Hot tea, Jimmy, with lots of sugar."

Jimmy smiled on top of his normal smile and sipped carefully at the hot tea.

Ian looked at me.

"He's in heaven."

"I can see that."

"Matt put us in the first row."

I wasn't surprised.

"It's nice to see you, Ian."

"It's nice to see you."

"Are you going to the reception tonight?"

"We're invited."

"Have you been thinking about me?" I asked.

He hesitated, then smiled.

"It's hard not to think about a girl who kisses you like that."

"Like what?"

He shrugged, as if it was obvious.

"Like when you're not expecting it."

I leaned forward and did it again. I kissed him on the lips, lingered a bit, then I turned around and walked away, disappearing into the crowd.

I was clearly out of my mind.

19. Kiss II

Friday, December 18th

[Remembrance of Ian MacIan:]

She did it again.

Look, we Scots are supposed to be a stoic lot, right? But how do you respond to something like that? Fortunately, I didn't have to respond because, just like the last time, she turned around and walked away.

But Jimmy saw it.

Which made me a bit nervous.

After all, we were a pair of confirmed bachelors, and I didn't know how he'd respond. It had me worried.

When I sat down next to him, he said:

"Revival kiss."

A lot of people have trouble understanding Jimmy, especially his more cryptic stuff, but it was rare that I was confused.

But now I was.

After all, *who* was being "revived"? Jimmy's always been fascinated by love stories, especially the kind that have some kind of "restorative" kiss. Like *Snow White*. Like *Sleeping Beauty*. The kiss that saves, the kiss that revives. The kiss that restores the lover from a death or a deathlike sleep.

One time, Jimmy was thumbing through one of my arty books, and he spotted a picture of Canova's famous neoclassical masterpiece *Amore e Psiche*, which the French, who've got the original in the Louvre and should have known better, call *Psyché ranimée par le baiser de l'Amour*.

Meaning *Psyche Revived by Cupid's Kiss*.

Jimmy called me over and showed me the picture, and I knew exactly what he was thinking.

"It's not what you think, Jimmy."

I hated to burst his balloon, but we've always been truthful with each other, so I told him the truth about the old story of Psyche and Cupid. How Psyche had got herself zapped with a "sleep of innermost darkness," a "corpse sleep," and how her lover had revived her back to life with a prick of one of his magical arrows.

Not with a kiss.

"But I'm sure he kissed her after he revived her," I assured him, "and *that's* what Canova's portraying in his sculpture."

He took it like a man.

"Still nice," he said.

"Still nice," I agreed.

Now we were sitting beside each other in the Lake Placid winter, and I wondered how I should attempt to get to the bottom of things.

I tried a direct approach.

"Who's getting revived, Jimmy?"

"Ian MacIan."

I wasn't sure *what* I was being revived from, but I didn't press it.

Jimmy wasn't finished.

"You need a love, Ian."

I was taken aback. We'd never talked about such things before.

"Do you, Jimmy?"

I was worried about what I might hear.

Very worried.

"I'm fine."

I felt nothing but relief. To use the old cliché, the weight of the world fell off my shoulders.

20. Whiteface Lodge

Friday, December 18th

"Bunny time."

It was Rickie.

Which wasn't exactly fair.

Matt, wearing two gold medals over his burgundy sweater, one for the 500, one for the 1000, was standing across the reception hall with the other medal recipients, also wearing burgundy USA sweaters. They were posing, rather casually, for two official photographers. When the flashes were over, the crowd of about two hundred friends, family, and fans applauded loudly. Immediately, Matt and his fellow champions were swarmed with fans.

Many of them seeking autographs.

Many of them pretty young girls.

The aforementioned "snowbunnies."

Rickie and I were sitting at our table, watching like everyone else.

"I know this sounds pretty stupid," Rickie

continued stupidly, "since he's an Olympic athlete, but I never noticed what a physical specimen Matty is."

I rolled my eyes.

"Sure, that doesn't sound stupid at all."

She ignored my sarcasm.

Rickie was enjoying herself. Everything. The races, the reception, the champagne, our room at the luxurious Whiteface Lodge.

Actually, our "suite."

"We've got a hot tub!" she'd screamed earlier.

We also had a cast-iron fireplace in the room and a spectacular view of the Adirondacks.

Whiteface was huge. A magnificent, rustic "lodge" in the midst of the Lake Placid woodlands, with handcrafted and hardwood furnishings, wood-beamed ceilings, tasteful chandeliers, and, apparently, hot tubs.

Tonight the place was "Christmased up." With lighted tall trees, wreaths and garlands, with Christmas music playing lightly in the background.

"I think he lied," I said, looking around the suite. "I think he paid for this place."

"Who cares? He's just trying to impress you. Why not enjoy yourself?"

Earlier at the oval, Matt had told Rickie that the room he'd reserved for us was "comped."

I had my doubts.

But maybe Rickie was right.

Maybe I should forget about everything and just enjoy myself.

I went to my bedroom, showered, primped, then dolled myself in a Carolina Herrera shirtdress. A fine red doupioni, flared, with a spread collar, button front, puffed short sleeves, and a hem to the knee. With cutely strapped black pumps.

"Whoa!" Rickie said.

You might have noticed that she says "Whoa" a lot. It's part of her plan to break herself of an unfortunate four-letter habit.

As for Rickie, she looked perfectly adorable and casual as always, with a pink knit sweater, a Prada knockoff, and tight white slacks.

Eventually, Matt extricated himself from the crowd and made his way toward our table.

"White Christmas" was playing.

Bing was singing.

Matt looked at me.

"Who's the prettiest girl in Placid?"

"Me," Rickie said.

"Second," Matt said, never shifting his eyes.

"Just Placid?" I kidded.

"In the universe."

I got a bit serious.

"I'm very proud of you Matt."

I knew how much he practiced and trained. How hard he worked. I knew about the relentless dedication, and I'd seen some of it "up close."

"That means more to me than these things."

He tapped his two medals.

Then three teenage girls approached, warily. All pretty, all respectful.

"Mr. Brooks?"

He turned to his fans.

"Can we have your autograph?"

"Of course."

He signed their programs, exchanging some skating banter.

It was lovely to watch.

"Some pictures too?" one of the girls asked.

"Sure, of course."

Then more girls arrived.

Matt looked at me, helplessly.

"Sorry, Polly. It'll be over soon. Can we talk later?"

"Of course."

"And dance?"

"Of course."

Satisfied, he leaned over and kissed me on the check, which was charming. Then he was led away by his fans for individual photos and more and more autographs.

"Snowbunny heaven."

Rickie seemed more amazed than cynical.

"It comes with the turf," I said.

She nodded and sipped her champagne.

Then I spotted Ian and Jimmy. Over at the buffet table.

"See those two over there?"

I pointed.

"Yeah."

I dug into my pocketbook and pulled out two fifties."

"We going to walk over there, and you're going to take Jimmy to the gift shop and buy him whatever souvenir he wants."

Rickie understood, and I put the money in her hand.

"I hope you know what you're doing," she said.

"I don't have the foggiest idea what I'm doing."

Five minutes later, Rickie walked off with Jimmy, and I looked at Ian.

"Let's go outside."

"You'll freeze."

"I'll get my coat and meet you there."

He shrugged.

I left him at the buffet, went to my room, grabbed my Canada Goose black parka, and met him on the empty veranda.

He was still wearing his jeans, his red flannel shirt, his green windbreaker.

His shades.

In the night.

"Where's your coat?" I said.

"I don't need one."

Which seemed ridiculous, but I didn't press it.

The night was clear, cold, and beautiful. Even romantic. We were surrounded by the high dark

Adirondacks, and off in the distance I could still see McKenzie Mountain. Faintly, I could also hear the Christmas music from the reception. It was "The Christmas Song." It sounded like Nat King Cole.

I didn't waste time.

"Did you get my letter?"

"I did. It was as lovely as you are, Polly Kinnell, but there was no need to apologize again."

"That's it?"

He seemed uncertain what to say.

He shrugged.

"It was nice to get a letter in today's world."

Which was a perfectly ridiculous thing to say under the circumstances, and I shook my head in frustration.

But I wasn't about to give up."

"Can you hear the music?"

"Of course."

I waited.

Nothing.

"Don't Scottish boys know when to ask a girl to dance?"

"I'd love to, Polly, but . . ."

He hesitated, even though he never seemed like the kind of guy who hesitated.

"But what?" I pressed him.

"There's something you need to know."

I waited.

It seemed like forever.

"I'm 'promised,'" he said.

Look, I'm doing my best to accurately record this absurd conversation, which I realize seems perfectly unbelievable.

By now, I was fully exasperated.

"What is this, Ian? The Eighteenth Century?"

He shrugged again, which was even more exasperating.

"Engaged?" I tried.

"Not really, just promised."

"By whom?"

"By me."

"Who is she?"

"We've known each other since grade school."

I looked into the sky. There were lots of stars and one big stupid fat moon. I stared at it like a moron. Then I got a hold of myself and looked back at Ian.

"I guess I've been a fool. After all, we don't even know each other."

"I know more than you think."

Since I didn't know what that meant, he gave me a taste.

"I know that you like Bruce Springsteen, Howie MacDonald's fiddle, and Gregorian chants. I know that you were a lit major at Columbia, a business minor, and an excellent writer. I know that you love mysteries, love stories, castles, ghosts, and Mexican food."

I was amazed.

Ian continued.

"I know you were homeschooled through the 12th grade, that you grew up in Scotch Plains, New Jersey, that you share an apartment in Manhattan with your best friend Rickie. I know you play a bit of tennis, that you stink at golf, that you love Graham Green novels, Austen novels, Rembrandt pictures, and, of course, I know what you do for a living."

I waited for an explanation.

"Your dad told me. With a lot more. He talked about you all the time."

I was amazed.

"Did you know him well?"

"Yes, especially those last four years on Skye. When your father was a young man he used to sing with my father who was well-known in the Highlands. It was my father who taught your dad the Gaelic style."

"Then we have old ties."

"Yes, we do. Your dad and my dad were very close friends."

It was comforting.

Ian wasn't finished.

"I hope you don't mind me pointing out the obvious, Polly, but Matt's a very special guy. And not because he wins skating medals."

I knew it was true.

"I know."

He looked back at the lodge.

"It's getting too cold. Maybe we should go back inside."

He didn't seem cold at all.

I didn't want things to end like this.

"Are you flying home through New York?"

"Yes, we're checking out the new pub site tomorrow morning."

"Take me."

He seemed hesitant.

"It's just an empty building, Polly, and I've got another boring appointment in the afternoon."

I stepped closer, looking into the stars gleaming off the surface of his shades.

"Give me tomorrow, Ian. And tomorrow night."

More hesitation.

"Don't over-think it," I said.

He gave in.

"Fine, it's Jimmy and me together."

"Of course."

We stood there still close in the night.

"Are you going to kiss me again?"

"No, it wouldn't be much of a surprise."

He smiled.

"You're quite a girl, Polly Kinnell."

Then he added:

"Miss Polly *Anna* Kinnell."

I was astonished. I'd never told anyone my middle name. My parents gave me the name because they loved the old Disney classic film *Pollyanna* with Haley Mills.

"Your father told me," he explained.

"Of course, he did."

I took him by the arm, and we went back inside the lodge.

21. New Sult Inn

Saturday, December 19th

"Let's check it out, Jimmy," Ian said, unlocking the door.

We were standing in front of the old Victoria Tavern on Macdougal Street just south of Washington Square. With its handsome large-stone front, big wooden doors, and a "Closed" sign in the window.

We'd just gotten out of our cab. A yellow one. Ubers were out of the question.

"Jimmy likes cabs," Ian explained earlier. "Yellow ones."

Fine.

Ian opened the doors, and we stepped inside. When I found the light switch, the place lit up. It was empty, but lovely. Wooden floors, wooden ceiling, wooden everything. Except for the stained-glass cabinets, polished brass, big stone fireplace, and period gaslights. It definitely had a Victorian ambiance. Jimmy made his way across the wooden floorboards and sat down on a stool in front of the ornately-carved mahogany bar.

"What do you think?" Ian asked Jimmy, who nodded affirmatively.

Ian looked at me.

"It's beautiful, Ian. Is it big enough?"

He pointed at the far wall.

"We're thinking about knocking out that wall, there's a small dining room on the other side."

He took out his notebook and tape measure, then started snooping around, eventually disappearing into the other rooms.

The office, the other dining room, and the kitchen.

I went over and sat next to Jimmy, who seemed to be having the time of his life. Both at Lake Placid and today in the city.

"Maybe we should practice," I suggested.

He wasn't sure what I meant.

"Let's start with a compliment."

It was instantaneous.

"You move like a goddess and look like a queen."

I laughed.

"You sure know how to make a girl feel good, Jimmy. How about another one?"

"Smiles are the language of love."

I smiled.

"I know some quotes too. All about chocolate. Would you like to hear a few?"

He nodded yes.

"Chocolate isn't a substitute for love. Love is a

substitute for chocolate."

His smile got bigger, even mischievous.

"More."

"Nine out of ten people love chocolate, the tenth person is a liar."

He laughed. It was more like a chuckle. A word I don't think I've ever used before.

"Your turn, Jimmy. Let's try some insults."

There was no hesitation.

"Your mother should have thrown you away and kept the stork."

How could I keep from smiling?

"Give me another one."

"I'm sorry you had so much trouble peeling your M&Ms."

"All right, Jimmy, let's pretend it's two lovebirds leaving the inn. No, let's make it even harder, let's make them newlyweds."

"What's the difference between a new husband and a new dog?"

I played along.

"What?"

"After a year, the dog is still excited to see you."

"All right, let's say it's a group of three."

He dipped into his endless mental repository and looked at me directly.

"You're clearly the smartest of the group, which is a little like calling Moe the smartest of the Three Stooges."

"All right, how about a flirty girl."

Ian came back in the room and listened.

"You've been on more laps than a table napkin."

I was amazed, as Ian stepped over.

"Where did you hear that?"

He was firm, but not castigating.

"Duncan Frasier."

"Well, don't ever say it again, Jimmy. It's crude."

Jimmy understood and nodded.

"And remind me when we get back home to give Duncan a knock on the head."

Jimmy nodded again.

I changed the subject.

"How's the kitchen?"

"Looks great, just give me a few minutes in the basement."

"Take your time."

Ian took off again and vanished.

"All right, Jimmy, how about one of those Scottish proverbs you like so much?"

"Be slow in choosing a friend, be slower in changing him."

I wondered if it was random.

"Ian tells me you like romantic comedies."

"Yes."

"Me too."

"Which ones?"

It was actually a long list, and I'd never attempted to rank them before. But I threw out a few of my favorites.

"*While You Were Sleeping, Sleepless in Seattle,* and *Return to Me.*"

He seemed pleased.

What's your favorite, Jimmy?"

No hesitation.

"*Just Like Heaven.*"

I wondered why, then I realized.

"Ghosts and love."

"Ghosts and love," he repeated.

I thought it over.

"You love my Ian," he said.

He said it matter-of-factly, and I was astonished. I didn't know what to say.

He wasn't finished.

"He loves you."

Now I was really flabbergasted. Another word I've never used before.

Then Jimmy moved things right along.

"I'd like a favor."

"Of course."

"Write me the love story."

"What love story?"

"About the Chocolate Princess."

"Me?"

"Yes. And the Ice Warrior. And the Graveyard Knight."

I tried to wiggle out of it.

"I'm not much of a writer, Jimmy."

"That's not what Ian says," he contradicted.

Since *whatever* Ian says seems to be the law of the land, I didn't bother to argue.

"Who are *you*, Jimmy?"

He understood.

"The Memory Boy."

It was hard not to smile.

He looked at me directly.

"Will you?"

"Yes."

"All of it?"

"Yes."

"Like *Persuasion*?"

As if it wasn't enough of a challenge, now I had to be the equal of Jane Austen.

"I'll do my best."

"Take your time."

Well, at least I wasn't under the gun.

"I'll be waiting."

Any possibility that the Memory Boy would forget about his promised "love story" was obviously impossible.

I had no idea, of course, how to actually do such a thing. Write a novel. But why not? I've always wanted to, and these days I wasn't doing anything else given that I was now tasteless and jobless. But I did realize that I needed to give him a warning.

A caveat.

"Not all love stories have happy endings, Jimmy."

"Like *Casablanca*?"

"Yes, like *Casablanca*."

It seemed to me that he'd never thought about the possibility.

He mulled it over.

"Fine," he decided.

That was that.

Ian was back.

Before I had a chance to ask Jimmy about Ian's "promised" bit. Now I'd have to wait for another opportunity.

"Everything OK?" I asked.

"Aye, it's looking very doable."

"Would you guys actually come to New York?"

"Sure."

I was astonished, but I didn't let on.

"Really?"

He seemed to recognize the misunderstanding.

"Sure, a weekend here, a weekend there."

I understood.

He explained further.

"I've got a job, Polly."

"Is it the money? I know I shouldn't ask."

He shook his head no.

"I know I shouldn't ask this either, but how much do you make digging graves?"

Jimmy butt in.

"Nothing."

I was stunned. Was Ian independently wealthy? He

certainly didn't live like it.

"Nothing?" I repeated stupidly.

Jimmy explained.

"It's a corporal work of mercy. Number seven."

Ian laughed and looked at his cousin.

"Somebody's quite the over-talkative lad this morning."

Then he checked his watch and changed the subject.

"We've got another appointment."

22. St. Anthony's Cemetery

Saturday, December 19ᵗʰ

I was back in another cemetery.

With my two "cemetery" boys.

"Lads."

Our yellow taxi slowly weaved its way through huge St. Anthony's in Westchester County north of the city. Even in the dead of winter, the grounds are beautiful. The graves stretched out forever over the lightly rolling hills, with an endless variety of tombstones, memorials, and white mausoleums.

This was Ian's "other appointment."

Naturally, I was worried how I'd react, especially given my troubled visits to the graves of my parents in Tarskavaig. But the "lads" were a comforting presence, and somehow, as we glided through the cemetery, I was able to relax. To appreciate the beauties of this amazing final resting place.

We pulled up to the door of the main office, and a man in a dark suit was waiting outside. He was

Nicholas Palmer, the CEO at St. Anthony's. He was a pleasant man in his mid-fifties, and he was delighted to see Ian.

And Jimmy.

After the men shook hands, Ian introduced me.

"This is our friend, Polly Kinnell."

"It's nice to meet you, Polly."

We shook hands, and Palmer looked at Ian.

"I hope she's more than a 'friend.'"

Ian ignored his teasing.

As for me, I had no idea what was going on.

As you've probably noticed, the Graveyard Knight isn't much of a talker. So when I heard that we were heading to a cemetery, I wondered if he was hoping to line up some part-time work for his eventual trips back to New York. But now it was clear that it was much more than that.

"How's everything," Ian wondered, "down on the northwest slope? Any problems?"

"None," Palmer assured him. "You did a great job."

Ian was silent but obviously pleased.

"Come inside, everybody," Palmer offered. "I've got lots of hot coffee."

The man was probably freezing in his blue suit.

Then he nodded at Jimmy.

"And lots of hot chocolate."

Ian looked at Palmer.

"Why not take Jimmy inside? I'd like to check a

few things. Give me twenty minutes or so."

Everyone was fine with that, including me.

Who still had no idea what was going on.

A few minutes later, Ian and I were walking around the cemetery. Mostly in silence.

I felt perfectly comfortable, and he seemed perfectly comfortable with me. I wished that he'd take my hand, but he didn't.

St. Anthony's seemed a lovely place for the dead. The grounds were impeccable, carefully laid out, and beautiful. Ian, from behind his black lenses, took everything in. Eventually, we came upon three diggers working near an open grave with a small backhoe. When they saw Ian, they stopped immediately and came up to the path. They were all Hispanic guys, in dirty work clothes. One was older, maybe mid-sixties. The younger guys were probably in their late thirties. As they approached, it seemed to me that the older man bowed slightly in Ian's direction, which was very peculiar.

Maybe I was mistaken.

He spoke with a pleasing Latin accent.

"It's wonderful to see you again, Mr. MacIan!"

He spoke with humble deference, with deepest respect.

They all shook hands, and I was introduced.

The old man looked at me and said softly:

"I will be at your service, señorita."

Which was lovely, yet odd, as if oddly phrased.

Ian looked over the grounds.

"The dead are happy here, Luis, because you treat them so well."

The old man was moved by the compliment. Honored and flattered.

Ian looked directly at one of the younger men.

"I've been thinking about you, Carlos. Have your griefs found any comfort?"

"As much as possible," the man explained. "She's never far from me out here."

Again, Ian seemed pleased.

I assumed that the poor man had lost his wife, or maybe his mother, and that she was buried right here at St. Anthony's.

"I'm off to check the northwest."

The men understood.

"It's perfect," Luis assured him. "You'll see."

"Good."

It seemed clear that the men didn't want him to leave.

"God bless you," Luis said.

As did the others.

"Sí, Dios te bendiga."

I heard one of the younger men mention *"el don,"* and the other one mention *"la bendición."* My Spanish is pretty lame, but I did know that *"el don"* is a "gift" of some kind. As for *"bendición,"* I googled the word later. It means a "blessing" of some kind.

The three men stepped forward, and each gently touched Ian on the arm. It was odd. Weirdly reverential. I didn't know what to make of it.

Soon Ian and I were once again walking the paths amid the tombstones.

"I guess someone's a celebrity gravedigger," I kidded, probably foolishly.

He smiled.

"My brother diggers."

Eventually, we arrived at a white-stone bench overlooking the northwest section of the cemetery. The endless graves stretched out before us, sloping down gradually toward a distant lake that was surrounded by a thick but leafless forest, except for the dark-green evergreens. It was spectacularly beautiful, perfectly peaceful.

We sat down, and I ran down the list, reciting out loud the seven "works" as I'd done for my mother as a child:

> *Feed the hungry*
> *Give drink to the thirsty*
> *Clothe the naked*
> *Shelter the stranger*
> *Visit the sick*
> *Bury the dead*

I looked at Ian.

"I've forgotten number six! My mother would be

horrified!"

He helped me out.

"'Ransom the captive.' It's an easy one to forget."

These are the seven "corporal works of mercy." The seven ways in which charity can be expressed "physically." According to Jimmy, number seven was why Ian did what he did, which seemed hard to believe.

"I suppose there's not much opportunity to 'ransom the captive,'" I said, "but there's tons of graves that need to be dug."

He knew what I wanted.

An explanation.

"That's right, Polly. It's what I do. What my father did before me, and his father before him."

It wasn't much of an explanation.

"Do you always use a shovel?"

"We've got a small backhoe for whenever I need it, but I prefer the shovel."

I looked at him and got sidetracked.

"What's with the shades?"

"Hypersensitivity to sunlight. I wear them at night because I'm used to them, and because I like to irritate pretty American girls."

"Let me see."

He took off his shades, and I looked into his eyes."

"They're lovely, Ian. They're brown."

"Like chocolate."

I laughed, and he put his shades back on, but I wasn't about to give up on the gravedigger "business."

"Why do you do it, Ian? I still don't get it."

It made him a bit uneasy, but he did his best.

"I would say it's a kind of reciprocity. A recompense. For the blessings in my life. It's become an obligation, a duty. I try to give comfort to the dead, and bury those who might not get a proper burial."

"Have you ever thought about giving it up?"

"Never."

"And you do it for nothing?"

"Yes."

"Then how do you and Jimmy survive? You can't live on a fiddler's pay."

He lifted his hand and waved it over the graves before us. Over his domain.

"This, Polly. I designed it."

Needless to say, I was astonished.

"From time to time, I design expansions like this one, and that more than provides for Jimmy and me. It gives us far more than we really need."

I wanted more.

"Help me out."

He did.

"I studied landscape architecture at university, at St. Andrews in Fife, and I was lucky enough to intern at an Edinburgh firm that specialized in designing golf courses. All over the world. So I learned a lot. And my dad taught me a lot."

I think it was the most I'd ever heard him speak about anything.

"You're quite an oddball, Ian MacIan."

"I suppose I might be. But someday, I'll be in my grave, and I hope I'll be comfortable. Jimmy too."

He looked at me.

"You too, Miss Polly."

"Well, before you go putting me in the ground, I've got something special planned for tonight."

He nodded.

Then shrugged.

We were back to that.

I fended off his silence.

"Tell me about Jimmy."

If I was going to write a story for Jimmy, I wanted to know my audience better.

So he told me.

23. The Roxie

Saturday, December 19th

He wasn't seventeen anymore, but Dion was still rocking the jam-packed Roxie:

> *Each night I ask the stars up above,*
> *Why must I be a teenager in love?*
> *Why must I be a teenager in love?*

We were sitting at a table near the stage. Jimmy was wide-eyed and spellbound, swaying slightly to the music.

It wasn't the old Roxy, now long gone, it was the "new" Roxie, dark, hip, and intimate. A perfect place to see Dion DiMucci.

Ever since my trip to Scotland, and my visit at Ian's cottage, I'd been listening to Jimmy's favorites.

Dion and Anne Murray.

Learning about them as well.

Dion DiMucci, who grew up in the Bronx, had

been a rock-and-roll sensation back in the late fifties and early sixties. A doo-wop sensation. Young American girls went totally nuts for his handsome good looks, his "Italian" good looks, and I've seen the old pictures. The girls were right.

He had a string of huge hits, including, most famously, "Runaround Sue" and "A Teenager in Love," the classic teenage lament. Then he went through some serious "changes," beat back some addiction issues, and came out the other side, still married to the love of his life. They now live down in Florida, partially retired, but he still does occasional concerts.

Like the Roxie tonight.

I'm so happy that Rickie spotted it. Jimmy's in heaven, and the rest of us were drinking tequila and having a rocking great time.

T-and-lime for Ian, Sunrises for Rickie, Palomas for me.

Dion wrapped "Teenager in Love," then broke into a wildly raucous r&r version of "Jingle Bells."

There was a reason why Springsteen idolized the guy. There was a reason why Bob Dylan once said that if you want to learn how to sing, listen to Dion.

Then he took a break.

"Thanks so much, everyone! Thanks again! We'll be right back after a little break. See you soon!"

I looked over at Ian and Rickie, as pre-planned, and held up my empty glass.

"I could stand another."

It was something my father used to say.

Tonight, it was the cue to Ian and Rickie, and they immediately stood up and melted into the crowd.

I turned to Jimmy.

"Having fun?"

"The best!"

I hated to break the Dion mood, but I knew that I might not get another chance to get Jimmy alone, and I needed some help.

I leaned closer in the loud Roxie.

"I was wondering, Jimmy. Who's Ian 'promised' to?"

He responded immediately.

"Heather MacDonald."

Which was certainly the most Scottish name I'd ever heard.

"What's she like?" I asked casually.

He shrugged.

I didn't give up.

"Don't you know her, Jimmy?"

"No."

I was astonished.

Jimmy wasn't finished.

"She lives at #1 Church Lane in Lochaline."

Then he looked at me and put his finger to his lips. As if he'd said something he shouldn't.

I wondered if I should keep pressing. Then his eyes lit up like saucers.

Not for me.

Rickie and Ian were back with their special "guest."

At Lake Placid, when I realized that Jimmy and Dion would be in the Village on the same night, I sent an email to the Roxy, with a note for Dion, asking if he could take a few minutes to say hello to Jimmy MacBride, his "biggest fan," who was visiting from Scotland. I really didn't expect it to work, especially on such short notice, but I got Dion's response email late last night:

Will do! At intermission.

Now Dion was standing right next to us.

He put out his hand to Jimmy.

"Hey, Jimmy, having a good time?"

"The best."

They shook hands.

"Ian told me you like 'Runaround Sue,' so I'll sing it for you later, OK?"

"OK."

"But now I've got to change this sweaty shirt and take a little rest. But I'll be back."

"The best," Jimmy repeated.

Dion winked at me, then took off. Ian and Rickie sat back down, and I took a hit off my new Paloma.

"Who did it?" Jimmy asked Ian.

"Polly."

He put his head gently on my shoulder for a

moment.

"That's how he says, 'thank you,'" Ian explained.

"You're welcome, Jimmy."

Four hours later, the four of us were standing in front of the Walker Hotel on 13th Street, north of the square. Standing in front of its handsome brick façade with its copper-clad bay windows and its old-fashioned gaslights.

Jimmy and Rickie were standing by the waiting cab. Rickie was doing her best to give me some privacy with Ian.

Who looked at me through his shades.

"It was a wonderful night, Polly. He'll never forget it. Neither will I."

I wondered if he'd kiss me. It was certainly his turn.

Nothing.

"Is that it?" I asked.

Ian shrugged, looking a bit helpless, but I wasn't about to let him off the hook.

Especially since I was reinforced with tequila courage.

"Tell me one thing," I said.

"All right."

"Tell me you don't love me."

There was no response.

Jimmy butt in.

"He does."

So much for privacy.

I looked over at Jimmy.

"Thank you, Jimmy."

Then I turned back to Ian and repeated myself.

"Tell me you don't love me."

There was a long pause in the cool winter night.

"I'm sorry, Polly, but I can't tell you that."

Then he leaned forward and kissed me.

On the forehead!

My damned forehead!

Then, along with Jimmy, he escaped into the entrance of the Walker.

Eventually, Rickie came over and guided me to the cab.

It was yellow, of course.

24. Kinnell's Manhattan

Thursday, December 24th

It was Christmas Eve.

Once again, I was wearing my elf hat.

The red one with the little white ball at the end.

I handed the elderly lady, Mrs. Morrison, a large white bag full of individually-prepared chocolate boxes.

Christmas presents.

She was one of our regulars, a "frequent flier."

"Thank you, my dear. The whole family loves your father's chocolates. May he rest in peace."

Rickie came into the store behind Mrs. Morrison.

I smiled at the older woman.

"Do you know why there's no such thing as Chocoholics Anonymous?"

She returned my smile, shrugged, and waited.

"Because no one wants to quit."

She actually laughed, but Rickie, who's heard all my chocolate jokes before, just rolled her eyes.

"Have a wonderful Christmas," I said, as the older woman began trudging toward the door.

"You too, my dear!"

Rickie held the door for Mrs. Morrison, then rushed back to the counter.

Excited.

"Guess what? Great news!"

I'm always ready for great news.

"The donation finally arrived!"

"Wonderful! How much?"

"Another fifty thousand!

"Fantastic!"

Rickie glanced around the empty store.

"Can you get out of here?"

I looked at the clock.

"Aunt Katie and her little Christmas helper should be back in about an hour."

"Fine. Meet me at the rink."

"See you there."

Rickie, as happy as could be, walked out to Fifth Avenue.

The store, which had been extremely busy all morning with last-minute shoppers, was suddenly silent. Except for Aunt Katie's Christmas music. It was Judy Garland singing "Have Yourself a Merry Little Christmas."

Which didn't seem possible this year.

Let your heart be light,
From now on your troubles will be out of sight.

I went back into the office, placing the chair so I could keep an eye on the front door.

Tomorrow was Christmas, but I felt little joy in my heart. For the first time in my life. I wasn't really moping, or bemoaning, but it's true I was definitely preoccupied. It was now five days since Ian had kissed me on the forehead and walked out of my life, and I was still thinking about him. Foolishly. Like a silly schoolgirl.

After all, I hardly knew the guy, and, let's face it, he's weird as hell, but I still couldn't get him out of my mind. I certainly didn't want to bore Rickie with it. Or worry Aunt Katie. So I kept it all inside and ruined these usually magical days before Christmas, when the world, when New York City, comes alive with a happy loving spirit.

I had no one to confide in, but I knew that there was someone else who was thinking about my situation.

You.

The Memory Boy.

Whom Ian had told me about on the bench in the cemetery.

Who'd asked me to write this story, *Casablanca* ending or not, which I started writing later that night. After the Roxie. After Ian walked away from me.

So here's what I know about *you*, whom I'm writing this for:

"Jimmy" James MacBride, the Memory Boy, came into this world seventeen years ago through a difficult birth. With an inexplicable brain hemorrhage, which he survived, which made him special. Special with certain problems, special with certain talents. He was, from birth, a memory "savant" who loved and memorized sayings, quotes, proverbs, maxims, adages, and epigrams.

Unfortunately, Jimmy is missing the memory that he'd like the most because his mother, Flora MacBride, who loved him above all things, died when he was a year old. But the boy was raised by a loving father, who also loved him above all things, who worked parcels for Royal Mail.

At their home in Castlebay on Barra in the Outer Hebrides, Jimmy was an only but happy child who never went to school. But his father taught him to read. And many other things. But, of course, nothing lasts forever in this life. Eight years ago, when Jimmy was seven, his father, James Michael MacBride of the MacDonald clan, died in a fluke platform accident, and Jimmy was immediately "taken in" by his beloved first cousin, Ian MacIan, who lives on the Island of Skye. Very quickly, Ian was designated as Jimmy's "official" guardian, and he's homeschooled Jimmy ever since. When Ian went off to study at the University of St. Andrews in Fife, he brought Jimmy along with him, and, later, he did the same when he worked in Edinburgh.

Jimmy, perpetually youthful, is now seventeen years old, and he works as a greeter at the Sult Inn on Sleat Peninsula. A job he loves. His cousin says that Jimmy, who has a consistently happy disposition, is the most beloved person on the Island of Skye. Only once was he ever treated badly, rudely, by an ignorant "out-of-control" drunken outsider from the Americas.

Jimmy loves love stories, ghost stories, rom-coms, castles, the Highland games, the Scottish hammer toss, speedskating, rugby, Dion DiMucci, Anne Murray, Celtic music, the pipes, the fiddles, and Celtic everything.

Quite recently, Jimmy's commissioned an autobiographical manuscript from Polly the Chocolate Princess regarding her pathetic love life.

I'm doing my best, Jimmy.

I looked at the picture of my father again, but I refused to cry. It was time to "man up."

"Woman up."

Burns only knew his Highland Mary for a month before they separated, and he lost her forever.

Which was a lot more tragic than my silly little crush on some guy I hardly knew.

Some guy who dug graves.

It was time to get over it.

I remembered Burns's farewell:

For there I took the last Fareweel
O' my sweet Highland Mary.

The bell at the front door jingled, and another last-minute customer entered into Chocolate heaven.

25. Rockefeller Center

Thursday, December 24ᵗʰ

We were sharing one of those huge, salty, doughy, slightly-burnt, slightly-warm NYC pretzels and watching the ice skaters glide effortlessly around the sunken rink at Rockefeller Center.

Not far from the world's most beautiful Christmas tree.

All around us, the hectic shoppers and meandering tourists were making their varied ways around and through the plaza.

It was lovely.

As was the music from the rink.

"Silver Bells."

One of my favorites.

City sidewalks, busy sidewalks,
Dressed in holiday style,
In the air there's a feeling of Christmas.

"Matt called," Rickie said, between bites. "He left you a message."

I wasn't surprised.

"Will you call him back?"

"Of course."

She looked at me closely.

"What am I going to do about you?"

"What am I going to do about myself?"

She laughed.

"Look, Polly, the guy's gone, and you haven't said a word about it, but I know what's going on."

I played along.

"What?"

"Ian."

Maybe it was a good time to put it to rest.

"He's got someone else, Rickie. He says he's 'promised.'"

She scoffed at the idea.

"What! What the hell does that mean? Even Italians don't 'promise' people anymore."

She was getting Bronx under the collar.

I shrugged, but she wouldn't let it go.

"Who is she?"

"Her name is Heather MacDonald. Jimmy says she lives in Lochaline, which is down in the Rough Bounds region."

"What else did he say?"

"Nothing. He doesn't know her."

Rickie was even more stunned, and more than a bit

irritated.

"That's ridiculous, Polly. How could Ian be engaged to someone who Jimmy's never met?"

"I have no idea, Rickie. I've been wondering the same thing."

She thought it over, deciding that it was time to give me some Rickie advice.

"Look, Polly, you've lost your dad, you've lost your job, and your store's in trouble. Now Matt's back, and you're obviously putting him off for some dopey fantasy about you-know-who, who's obviously giving you a line of crap."

I couldn't argue with any of it.

She continued advising, beginning with another Rickie "look."

"Look, honey, I like the guy, but this is nuts."

I turned and faced her, then I dropped the ball in her court.

"So what should I do?" I asked. "What would *you* do?"

"You really want to know?"

"Of course."

"I'd fly back to Scotland tonight and figure things out once and for all."

"It's Christmas Eve!"

"So what?"

I thought it over.

She had additional instructions.

"I'd start with his Highland Mary."

Meaning his Highland Heather.
Why not?

26. Lochaline

Friday, December 25th

More mist.

I hadn't even reached Skye yet.

I was badly lagged after my red-eye to Heathrow and my connection to Glasgow. I was also wondering if I was out of my mind.

My Scottish taxi driver, Lachlan MacCrory, maybe sixty or so, was less-than-carefully zipping along a heavily-wooded road above the ocean. Above the Sound of Mull, through the mountains of Morvern Peninsular. I'm sure he was looking forward to eventually getting back home to his family on Christmas Day, but he'd offered to stay with me as long as as needed.

I think he felt sorry for me.

Lochaline's very remote, a scattering of isolated houses, shrouded, of course, in Scottish mist.

Lachlan suddenly made a right turn onto a dirt road, and, immediately, we were surrounded by winter forest. Eventually, we drove through an open iron gate to the front door of a handsome ivy-covered stone structure.

In the middle of nowhere.

It didn't seem right.

"Are you sure this is 1 Church Lane?"

"Aye, Miss Polly, this is the one."

"Can you wait for me?"

"I'll be doing whatever you need."

"Thanks so much."

I left my travel bag on the back seat, got out of the taxi, and walked to the entrance.

There was a large wooden cross on the door and a bronze plaque:

Servants of St. Margaret

What?

What have I gotten myself into?

I knocked on the door.

"Come in, dearie. The door's ajar. Enter the room to your right."

"Ajar"?

There was obviously some kind of intercom above the door, but I couldn't see it.

Maybe a camera as well.

Oh, well.

I went inside and took the right into a little waiting room with wood-paneled walls, a single red poinsettia, and several striking religious icons. At the opposite end of the room, there was an iron grating. It seemed to me I was in some kind of cloistered convent.

Which made no sense.

An elderly nun appeared behind the iron grating. She wore a full black habit, with a loving smile on her face.

"A blessed Christmas, my dear. What can we do for you this wonderful morning."

Her brogue made Ian's sound like the Queen's English.

"I'm looking for Heather MacDonald."

She thought it over.

"Is it a bad time?" I wondered.

Of course, it was a bad time!

It was Christmas Day in a cloistered convent!

"Not a bit, young lady. She's rather handy."

I was hoping that "handy" meant "nearby."

When she vanished, I stared at the icons, mostly the one in which a kindly woman in nun-like robes was giving loaves of bread to the poor.

"That's Queen St. Margaret," a lovely voice said.

My mother, of course, had made sure that I knew all about the pious wife of Malcolm III, king of the Scots. Known as the "Pearl of Scotland," Margaret died near the end of the Eleventh Century. She was renowned for feeding the poor, especially orphans, every day before eating anything herself.

I turned around and looked through the grate.

She was a much younger nun, also in full habit, with the most beautiful face, with the most beautiful green eyes I've ever seen.

Lustrous.

Like emeralds, yet softer.

Behind her, the older nun sat in a chair, as a kind of silent chaperone.

"Are you Heather?" I asked.

The young nun smiled.

"Once I was. I'm now Sr. Marie."

I didn't know how to explain myself.

"I've come about Ian MacIan," I tried.

She seemed to understand.

"Have you fallen in love with him?"

She said it with concern.

With compassion.

"That's what I'm trying to figure out. He says he's been 'promised.' To you."

She wasted no time.

"We were young sweethearts. When we were sixteen, Ian made a silly vow to marry me someday. It was quite charming at the time."

"What happened?"

"Ian went off to college, and we fell apart, and I realized that I had another calling. There was nothing traumatic about it, and Ian always supported my vocation."

"Do you still love him?"

She thought it over.

"I suppose I do, but with a different kind of love. *This* is where I want to be, and *this* is what I love the most."

She was perfectly clear, but she wanted to be even clearer.

"Can I ask your name?"

"Polly Kinnell."

"Such a lovely name."

"High praise from Heather MacDonald."

She laughed, then she got serious again.

"A vow, Polly, is a very serious and binding thing, but the one Ian made is categorically nullified because the conditions under which he took his vow no longer exist. Clearly, I'm unable and unwilling to marry. So it's just an excuse of some kind."

I didn't know what to say.

"I'm sorry, Polly. It's not at all like Ian to be disingenuous."

"Yeah, that's what I thought. Do you have any idea what's going on?"

"I'm afraid I don't, Polly. But Ian's a 'digger,' and it might relate to his obligations. Maybe even his gift."

There was that "gift" again.

"Nobody's explained it to me."

"It's hard to explain."

"Please try."

She did her best.

"Because of what Ian does with his life, he has a special communion with the dead. Many people believe that his prayers for the dead are particularly efficacious. Some even believe that, on rare occasions, he has the power to reanimate someone at the brink of death."

The older nun spoke up, trying to be helpful.

"But only once in a lifetime, my dears. With the one exception."

I waited for more.

Sr. Marie explained.

"A digger can never save the person he's closest to."

It was hard to comprehend.

"It all sounds nuts. Is it really true?"

"Maybe not, who knows? But those are the legends of the 'diggers.' As for me, I believe that God often works in strange seemingly-illogical ways."

I thought it over.

I also thought of my cab driver sitting outside on Christmas Day.

"Are you happy here, sister?"

"Very much, Polly. Don't worry about me. I'm right where I want to be. Right where I *should* be."

I traded "Merry Christmas!" with both of the sisters and started for the door. Then I thought of something else and turned around.

"Have you ever been seriously sick?"

She knew what I was getting at.

"Nothing life-threatening, Polly. Ian never cured me if that's what you're thinking."

I nodded my thanks and left.

27. St. Mary's

Friday, December 25th

There was a Christmas wreath on the door.

First a convent.

Now a rectory.

From within, I could hear an odd repetitive sound. Like cracking.

Like smacking.

I knocked.

Lachlan MacCrory was waiting in his taxi reading a rugby magazine. He needed to get to his sister's house in Fort William by four o'clock, and we were still on schedule.

It was 11:11.

I was surprised that I wasn't as exhausted as I should have been. Lachlan said I was obsessed with the "need to know," with the need to get to the bottom of things. Which he certainly approved of. He was a rugged old-guy Scot, a widower, with Highland stoicism stamped indelibly on his tough-guy wrinkled face, but underneath the façade he was a lot of mush. Another closet romantic. I told him my whole stupid story on our drive from Glasgow to Lochaline, after my crack-of-the-dawn Christmas Mass in Glasgow, then I answered all of his follow-up questions on the ride to Skye.

He was "all in" for whatever I was doing, and I loved him for it.

It was starting to snow.

Oh, well. Who doesn't love a white Christmas?

When no one answered the door, I went inside and followed the cracking noise to the same white waiting room where I'd spoken to Fr. Buchanan last October. The one with the huge crucifix.

I entered the room.

It was quite a sight.

The old priest, who claimed he was 102 years old, still dressed in his white collar and priestly blacks, was skipping rope in the middle of the room. Vigorously. *Too* vigorously. When he saw me, he nodded, but he didn't stop.

He spoke in a winded staccato as he jumped.

"A few more. 96, 97, 98, 99, 100."

He stopped, smiled, and tried to catch his breath. Then he placed his jump rope on top of a chair and picked up a small white towel and began wiping his soaked forehead.

"There's still a bit of life left in the old dog!"

Was I more astonished, or more impressed?

I'm not sure.

I repeated what he'd said back in October.

"Good genes and exercise."

He laughed.

"Aye, pretty Polly."

When he'd caught his breath, he pulled over two chairs and we sat down facing each other.

"So why's the bonnie lass from New York City back on my island? Especially on the glorious day of Christmas?"

I didn't waste time. Lachlan was waiting in his taxi, and I'm sure the priest had his Christmas duties.

"I've been to see Sr. Marie in Lochaline, and I know about Ian's 'vow.' I've also heard the rumors about his 'gift.'"

The old priest shrugged, continuing to towel his face.

"Well, the vow's perfect nonsense, Polly. No longer in effect, and Ian knows it. As for his gifts, if he really has such things, they come with certain drawbacks and great responsibilities."

I cut to the chase.

"Can a digger like Ian really cure someone who's deathly ill? Maybe even dead?"

"Of course, he can't. Only God can do that. But God can cure, even revive, through the intercession of someone else. As has happened."

"Well, I've got my suspicions about that, father. Maybe Ian 'cured' someone in his past, or *thinks* that he did, and now he's convinced, for some reason, that it might come undone. Is that possible?"

"I don't see how."

"What about Jimmy?"

"Jimmy's problems go back to his birth, when he was knocking on heaven's door. But never since, as far as I'm aware."

I was even more confused than before.

The old priest looked at his watch.

"I'm sorry, Polly, but I've got midday Mass. I'm certain things will become clearer in time."

He stood up, and I did the same. Reluctantly. I was feeling desperate.

"The sisters told me that he can cure anyone except the one closest to him."

It was a question.

"Assuming he *really* can do such things, Polly," he said cautiously.

As we walked to the front door, he tried to be more helpful.

"It's actually closer than that, Polly."

I didn't understand.

"What do you mean?"

He looked at me directly.

"A 'digger' can never cure his own spouse, as Ian's grandfather found out."

I was amazed.

"Now you need to talk to the one."

It was clear that the "one" was Ian.

I nodded.

He raised his right hand and made the sign of the cross across my forehead with his thumb.

"Merry Christmas, my dear!"

Then he was gone.

28. Cottage

Friday, December 25th

We weaved through Tarskavaig Cemetery, through the falling snow, and I thought of my parents. Foolishly hoping they weren't cold in their side-by-side graves. Up ahead, I could see the cottage. Actually, I could see the outline of the cottage. Outlined in colorful Christmas lights.

Something dawned on me.

Something terrible.

What if they weren't alone on Christmas Day?

What if Ian and Jimmy were with another woman? Something which I'd never even considered in Rockefeller Center, in Heathrow, in Glasgow, in Lochaline. How could I be so foolish? I flushed with the painful adrenaline burn of stupidity, of potential humiliation.

After all, what was I doing anyway? I was acting like a pathetic teenager. With a childish crush. Should a modern woman really pursue a man like this? Did it make me weak? Make me needy? Or did it make me strong and assertive. A determined young woman who isn't certain what she wants but who's willing to go through all kinds of difficulties to figure it out.

I had no idea.

The jury was out.

But it helped that it was all Rickie's bright idea.

"Pull over, Lachlan!"

"You sure, missie? The snow's still coming."

"Please."

When he did so, I thanked him profusely for all his help, and I gave him the largest taxi tip ever given by someone without a job.

I grabbed my travel bag, stepped into the snow, as he rolled down his window.

"Have a happy Christmas, Lachlan."

"You as well, Miss Polly. My Christmas wish is that you'll find the love you deserve. If it's not here on Skye, then the lad's a damned fool, and you should be glad to fly back to America."

I leaned in the window and kissed him on the forehead.

Maybe it would be my only Christmas kiss.

As he turned his taxi around, I walked up the narrow snow-covered road to the front of the cottage.

Jimmy was sitting on the front porch. He was warmly dressed, with a dark wool cap and a familiar smile.

His smile made me very comfortable with my life.

"Bonnie Polly!"

"Merry Christmas, Jimmy!"

"And you."

There was a peculiar looking vehicle in the driveway.

"Is that thing an ambulance?"

It was painted dark blue.

Before Jimmy could answer, Ian came out the front door. He was dressed as he was always dressed. Open leather coat, a flannel shirt, a baseball cap, and shades.

My heart did something active in my chest.

"Ah, Jimmy boy," he said, "I see that Christmas is even more special this year."

He came down the steps.

He seemed pleased to see me, and he answered my question.

"Yes."

Meaning "yes" the thing in the driveway *is* an ambulance. Or, at least, it once was. Before the dark-blue paint.

So I got right to it.

"It's Christmas Day, and I've come for my present."

He waited.

"I want you to take me to Duntulm Castle."

He laughed, but he didn't dismiss it.

Duntulm was the place where my father met my mother.

Where they fell in love.

"Jimmy and I," he explained, "might get called to Inverness later this afternoon, but we can go to Duntulm first. Assuming we don't get snowed in."

"I'm told you're impervious to the cold, and I'm wearing Canada Goose."

"Fine."

He looked at Jimmy.

"How's that?"

"Better than fine."

29. Duntulm Castle

Friday, December 25th

The snow had stopped.

For the time being.

Everything was dark and overcast and eerily beautiful.

Jimmy was sitting on a large rock in the scattered rubble at the edge of the ruins of Duntulm Castle. High atop the seaward cliffs.

A few minutes earlier, Ian had brushed the snow off the rock, smiling mischievously, looking at Jimmy and me.

"I'll be back."

Then he was gone, heading down toward the nearby hotel, an old hunting lodge that boasted "the most spectacular views in Scotland." Which was quite a boast.

Naturally, I assumed the place was closed on Christmas Day.

So it was just Jimmy and me.

The Memory Boy, of course, already knew the history of Duntulm. Much better than me, I'm sure. But a few nights ago, in Manhattan, Rickie caught me typing in my bedroom in the middle of the night. She knocked on my door and came inside, warm in her nightgown, drowsy and confused.

I was worried that I'd woken her up.

"Did I arouse the dead?"

"No, but what the hell are you doing? It's three in the morning."

So I told her.

Why not?

"Jimmy asked me to write him a love story."

"What love story?"

"Me and Ian."

She was expressionless.

"Is it *really* a love story? I thought it was a disaster."

"Many love stories are disasters. *Romeo and Juliet*."

She laughed.

"Fine. I want to read it."

"Fine."

"Goodnight, Juliet."

"Goodnight, Rickie."

She turned around and left the room.

So now I'm writing for an audience of two, and I'll need to explain a few things that Rickie wouldn't know. After all, she knows next-to-nothing about

Scotland except for my bad behavior at the Sult Inn.

The ancient ruins of Duntulm Castle sit high at the north end of Skye over the ocean. The MacDonalds built the castle in the Fourteenth Century and abandoned the place in the 1700s when they moved to Armadale Castle at the southern end of the island. The view from the ruins is legendary, high above the rugged coast, with little Tulm Island and the hills of Harris off in the distance.

Oh, yeah, the place is riddled with ghosts.

At least four.

As my father once explained, there's "Weeping" Margaret, Donald Gorm, "Raving" Hugh MacDonald, and, most significantly, the "shrieking" nursemaid.

I mentioned the four ghosts to Jimmy.

"Nursemaid?" he asked.

I was surprised.

"Don't you know?"

He shook his head.

"No. Tell me."

So I told him, as best I could, remembering what my father had once told me.

Almost four hundred years ago, a young nursemaid was holding the infant child of the MacDonald chieftain in her arms. Then something went wrong. Maybe she slipped. Maybe she tripped. Whatever happened, she dropped the baby, and it fell down the cliffs and smashed to the rocks below. The chieftain was so distraught that he abandoned the castle, but before he did, he tied the nurse in a little boat and set her adrift on the ocean. To die a terrible death.

I finished my gruesome tale as Ian reappeared, holding a small white bag.

"So the shrieking nursemaid," I explained, "still haunts the ruins, wailing hysterically, just like the day she dropped the baby."

When Jimmy clapped a bit, I felt good about myself.

I looked at Ian.

"I'm surprised he's never heard that story."

He explained.

Honestly.

"I've never told him about the nursemaid because I didn't want him to have nightmares."

I was horrified.

What had I done?

Then Ian smiled and looked over at Jimmy.

"But he's a big lad now. Right, Jimmy boy?

Jimmy nodded.

Then Ian stepped forward and handed his cousin a small bowl of chocolate ice cream with a small spoon.

"Here's something from Doris down at the hotel. She said to tell you, 'Happy Christmas!'"

Jimmy's eyes lit up.

"Ice cream?" I said. "Outside? In December?"

Ian just shrugged.

"The only thing crazier than a Scotsman," I

pointed out, "is another Scotsman."

He didn't disagree.

As for Jimmy, he was absorbed in his treat.

Ian looked at him again.

"We're taking a little walk. OK, Jimmy?"

Jimmy nodded.

"And don't go anywhere," Ian said firmly.

Jimmy nodded again, and Ian looked at me.

"I want to show you something."

We walked off together, around the edge of the ruins, careful in the light snow.

Careful also to keep Jimmy in sight.

Then Ian stopped, above the cliffs.

"This is where it happened."

Where Angus Kinnell proposed to Bonnie Jean MacDonald.

"Your father once told me the spot," he explained, "but I've never heard the whole story."

So I told him.

"There was some kind of MacDonald gathering down in Kilmuir at the grave of Flora MacDonald. Afterward, my mother and my father met up here in the ruins."

"It's very romantic."

I was wishing that Ian would be a little more romantic himself, but I changed the subject.

"I talked to Sr. Marie earlier today."

He didn't seem surprised.

"And Fr. Buchanan too. We talked about 'vows'

and 'diggers' and 'gifts.'"

He smiled.

"Don't believe everything you hear, Polly. The Scots are a suspicious lot."

"I don't care, Ian. I don't care about *any* of it. All I want to know is one simple thing. Why you didn't answer my question in New York."

He knew what I meant, but he didn't respond.

"Look at me, Ian."

He did. Through his dark lenses.

"Just tell me you don't love me, and I'll go back to New York City, and that'll be the end of it."

"I'm afraid I can't do that, Polly."

I wasn't sure what he meant.

Then, unexpectedly, his cell went off, and I was startled. I stepped backward, slipping toward the edge of the cliffs. Instantly, Ian reached out, grabbed me, and pulled me toward him.

My heart was crashing. I was terrified.

"What am I doing?" I said stupidly.

"You slipped," he said, just as stupidly.

"My mother slipped that day too, and my father grabbed her. Right here."

I was never one for putting much stock in "signs," but maybe I was about to start.

"You're safe now, Polly."

Now, dearest Jimmy, in a love story like this, shouldn't, at such a magical moment, the dumb Scotsman get the hint and hold me tight and kiss me the greatest kiss in the history of the world, then sweep me away to his castle?

But he didn't.

Instead, he looked down at his cell.

"I hope it's really important," I kidded, trying not to sound too sarcastic.

"It is," he said seriously. "We need to go to Inverness. Right now."

"Fine. But I have a question."

He waited.

"Why don't *you* kiss me for a change?"

But he was distracted. He was staring over at Jimmy, so I looked as well. Jimmy was standing in front of his rock, crying like a child.

It broke my heart.

"He must have thought you were falling over the edge."

"I was."

We both rushed over and did our best to reassure and comfort Jimmy.

All of which, of course, was my fault.

30. Inverness

Friday, December 25th

It was snowing again.

We were driving A87 heading to Inverness in Ian's dark-blue ambulance. Driving in silence. Jimmy was sleeping between us in the front seat. He was resting his head on my shoulder, and I had my arm around him.

"Is he all right?" I whispered.

"Yeah," Ian assured me, not whispering, but speaking softly. "Jimmy's got the best disposition of anyone on the planet, but he can get scared sometimes. Really scared. Fortunately, he gets over it quickly."

I got worried.

"Did the shrieking nursemaid have anything to do with it?"

Ian smiled.

"Not at all. Jimmy thought you were falling off the cliff."

Satisfied, I switched directions.

"Am I making a fool of myself, Ian?"

"I doubt you could ever do that."

Which was nice of him to say, but hardly accurate given my landmark performance at the Sult Inn last October.

"Do you know why I'm here?" I asked.

"Yes."

I was surprised.

"Why?"

"Because you're trying to figure us out."

I laughed a bit, but I liked the "us."

"Is that why I flew 3,000 miles, drove into the Highlands, talked to a nun and a priest, and am currently sloshing through the snow in a ridiculous old ambulance?"

"Yes."

"Fine," I said. "Would you like to know what I think?"

"I can't wait."

"I think, against better judgement, that *you* think that you really did cure somebody sometime in the past, somebody like Jimmy, and you think that being with me will undo it somehow."

There was dead air.

For a long time.

Finally he turned to me.

"All right, Polly."

Very carefully, he pulled the car over to the side of the road, got out, came around my side, and opened the door. I guess it was time to finally settle things. Gently,

I extricated myself from Jimmy and stepped into the lightly falling snow. Ian shut the door as quietly as possible, and we walked to the front of the car, into the headlights.

Ian faced me, and his shades looked directly into my eyes.

Then he told me.

"Seven years ago, when I was nineteen, an old friend of my father's called me from New Jersey and asked me to fly to America because his daughter had been busted up in a car crash."

I was amazed.

"Me?" I said foolishly.

"Yes. I drove to Glasgow, flew to Newark, went to the hospital, and prayed the 'digger's prayer.' Then I flew back home."

I was silent, trying to figure out what it meant.

"There's more, Polly."

I waited.

"I've loved you from the moment I saw you twelve years ago."

I was confused once again.

He explained.

"It was long before my trip to the New Jersey hospital. Back when you were a young girl. Thirteen years old. At the Highland Games in Cowal. I was sixteen at the time, and I was competing, for the first time, in the hammer toss. In the junior division. I looked over, and I saw your family standing with my father and rooting me on. You were holding your mother's hand and watching me intently. I can't explain what I felt, Polly, and I tried to ignore it."

He smiled.

"Heather was there, and she kidded me about it later. 'Some dopey Scot just got himself smitten by a little Yankee girl.' So I kidded her right back, 'Aye, and now the vow's moot and dead,' and she laughed. But I still thought about you all the time. Then your father called me to New Jersey, and it seemed like a sign. A sign that it shouldn't happen. That you and I should never happen. Then your father came home to Skye, and he talked about you all the time."

"Did you ever tell him how you felt?"

"Never, it was pointless. Yes, I loved every single thing your father told me about his bonnie girl in New York City, but sometimes I wanted to tell him to shut up and leave me alone."

"Because you think that if we're together, if we're ever married, it'll all come undone?"

He shrugged.

I was perplexed to say the least.

"What do *you* think's going to happen, Ian?" I asked. "That I'll vanish into thin air? That I'll drop dead at the altar?"

It seemed preposterous.

He shrugged and said nothing.

"God would never allow such a thing!" I said, speaking on behalf of the almighty.

"God gives us a life of trials," Ian reminded me. "My own grandfather couldn't save his dying wife."

"Well, I don't believe it. *Any* of it. And I don't care. Let's just live our lives, Ian."

He went silent again.

"Do you know," I continued, "what I want for Christmas?"

"You've already got your present," he kidded.

"Do you know what I want for my other present?"

"Maybe I do."

"Then think about it."

"I think about little else."

"Then tell me you love me."

"I do, Polly. I love you. I've loved you for twelve years."

It was over.

Finally.

He leaned down and kissed me tenderly. It was the happiest moment of my life.

Which I would never say lightly.

Then we heard a racket from the front seat of the car, and we looked over, and the Memory Boy was clapping.

Smiling.

31. St. Anthony's

Friday, December 25th

"A hospital?"

I was confused once again.

After our kiss in the snow, we got back in the car, Jimmy immediately conked out, and we drove in silence through the Highland night. Me thinking of Ian, and him surely thinking of me.

Eventually, we arrived at our destination in Inverness. Ian pulled his old ambulance close to the entrance of St. Anthony's Hospital.

"Aye."

That was a big help.

Jimmy was rousing himself, staring at the entrance.

"Who are we visiting?" I wondered, wondering whom I should be concerned about.

"Three," Jimmy said.

"Three?" I repeated.

Soon I found out.

We made our way through the silent mostly-deserted hallways of the hospital. Occasionally, Ian would wave to a nurse at a distant desk, and she'd yell out "Merry Christmas, Ian!" Then we'd continue through even darker and more isolated hallways until we entered a room that smelled different than the rest of the hospital.

Not a very likeable smell.

Great!

Inside, there were three bodies laid out on wheeled tables, covered to the neck with white sheets.

I looked at Jimmy.

"Is this what I think it is?"

Which was pretty obvious.

"Aye."

Ian was off talking to the morgue attendant, a tired but friendly woman in her late forties who was holding a clipboard.

She said what all the others said.

"Merry Christmas, Ian!"

"Yes, it's that, Kathleen."

Then she pointed at the middle corpse, an old man.

"I'm afraid we don't have a name for this one. They found him in an alley in Aberdeen."

Ian nodded.

"If you'll sign a few things," she continued, "I can get home to my husband."

They walked over to a nearby counter and completed the forms together. In the meantime, Jimmy and I stared at the dead. Jimmy seemed very comfortable, but I was creeped out. Totally. Sure, I've been to a few wakes before, but never inside a morgue.

All three of the dead were old, worn out, and haggard. Two men and a woman. Maybe drinkers. Maybe druggers.

"Who are they?" I asked Jimmy.

He answered as if by rote.

"The destitute, the homeless, the unclaimed."

I understood.

"So Ian's taking them back to Skye to bury them?"

"Aye."

32. Eilean Donan

Friday, December 25th

Twenty minutes later, all six of us were driving back on A87. Three in the front seat with three body bags stretched out in the back.

"How you doing?" Ian asked.

"I'm good. They're all very well behaved."

He smiled and looked at the dashboard clock.

"I've been thinking about what you wanted me to think about," he said. Then, as if to himself, "It's almost eleven o'clock."

I had no idea what the time had to do with anything, so I watched in silence as he pulled his cell, speed-dialed a number, set it on speaker, and placed it on the dashboard in front of us.

It rang twice as Jimmy roused himself from his drowsiness, wondering like me what was going on.

Someone picked up at the other end.

"Ian?"

It was Matt's voice.

"Can I ruin your Christmas?"

Matt seemed to understand.

"Only if it'll make her happy," he answered on speaker.

"We've talked about this, right? About the possibility."

I was amazed.

The two of them sounded like old friends.

"I know," Matt responded, "and I still stand by what I said."

"Can I have your permission to ask?"

"Yeah, I meant it then, and I mean it now. Is Polly there?"

"Aye, right beside me. We're driving back from Inverness with Jimmy."

"With the dispossessed?"

"Three unwanteds."

There was a pause.

"Well, tell her I love her, in case she says 'no.'"

I was overwhelmed.

I said nothing.

"She heard you," Ian said.

"Well, let me know what happens. I hope she says 'no.'"

I felt that I should say something, but what can you say at a moment like that? "Thanks, Matt"? "God bless you, Matt"? I had no idea, so I did what I usually did, I said something stupid.

"I wish I was twins."

He laughed at the other end.

"Merry Christmas to the weirdo lovebirds," he finished. "Merry Christmas to Jimmy."

"Matt Brooks is the best."

Jimmy was right.

Ian and Matt hung up.

Fully satisfied that all was right in the world, Jimmy put his head on my shoulder and went off to drowsyland again, as silence overwhelmed the ambulance. Lots and lots of stuff was cluttering my mind, and I lost track of the time. I lost track of reality. Eventually, Ian turned off the main road, and there in front of us was Eilean Donan, often called the most beautiful castle in Scotland. I'd seen it in my picture books, of course, but no picture could capture the magic of this Scottish fantasy.

Ian drove to the small bridge over Loch Duich, and I stared wide-eyed, like a child, at the amazing medieval castle, lit tonight with lovely white lights. Christmas lights. I could also hear a fiddle in the distance and the caroling of a small group that was standing near the front of the castle.

Singing "O, Holy Night."

My favorite.

"Do you know where we are?" Ian asked.

"Yes, Eilean Donan. I've known about it since I was a child."

Named for a Celtic saint, the castle was first built in 1220 to protect the area from Viking raiders.

Associated with the Mackenzies, then the MacRaes, it was built and rebuilt over the years and almost destroyed during a Jacobite uprising in 1719. Final restorations began in 1912.

The castle sits on a tiny island at the northern end of Loch Duich, and it's only connection to the mainland is a footbridge. It's the "most photographed" castle in Scotland, and it's hard to imagine anything more striking, more dramatic, more romantic.

The snow and the lights didn't hurt.

Neither did the music.

Before we got out of the car, Ian looked at me directly, above resting Jimmy.

"If somebody says 'yes' tonight, I want her to talk to Dr. Cooper in New Jersey."

I wasn't sure what he was talking about. Probably relating to my accident seven years ago and Ian's visit.

Maybe they knew each other.

"Sure."

"Promise me, Polly."

"I promise."

We coaxed Jimmy awake.

Then Ian took my hand, and we walked across the little footbridge with Jimmy beside us.

Eilean Donan has thousands of visitors each year, but I felt certain that we were the only ones with three dead bodies in the car.

A few minutes later, we were standing within a group of about fifty spectators listening to an old fiddler and twelve carolers finishing "O, Holy Night." It was lovely, and we all clapped, including Jimmy. The Christmas performance was over and the spectators began to leave. Then Ian walked over to the old fiddler. It was obvious that they knew each other.

Fellow fiddlers.

When Ian came back, he took my hand and looked at Jimmy.

"Wait here, lad, and see if I do it just right."

Jimmy nodded, as Ian led me to a spot closer to the walls of the castle, lit with small white lights.

Immediately, he knelt down in the snow in front of me.

He even took off his shades.

This was serious!

He looked up.

At me.

"If you say yes, I'll dedicate my whole life to your happiness. Will you marry me, Polly Kinnell?"

"Yes."

"When?"

I didn't think. I just answered.

"Next Christmas."

"Perfect."

It was over.

Whether rash or not, it was over.

Ian stood up and nodded to Jimmy, who was clapping enthusiastically. As were the carolers and the fiddler. Then my fiancé kissed me, and we embraced.

Immediately, the fiddler started playing a tune, as the carolers began to sing Anne Murray's beautiful love song, "Can I Have This Dance (For The Rest of My Life)."

"Can I have the dance I didn't have in Lake Placid."

"It's about time."

We danced.

He was far more graceful than one might expect from a gravedigger and a hammer tosser.

I wasn't so bad myself.

I was in heaven.

An otherworldly state.

We danced within the lights and the light snow.

When the song ended, we walked back over the footbridge with Jimmy. Behind us, the fiddler was playing "Loch Loman."

How lovely.

Ian MacIan was off to a hell of a start!

33. Dance

Friday, December 25th

[Remembrance of Ian MacIan:]

What have I done?

What have I undone?

One thing's for sure, I've done exactly what I've been trying to avoid doing for the last twelve years.

Something that I've kept in my heart.

Something that I never even told my father, or Angus, or even Jimmy.

Beginning at the Highland Games.

I was sixteen back then, big for my age, with a teenage sweetheart, and an untroubled life. I'd already accepted my apparent "fate" as a gravedigger, just like my father, just like his father before him.

"You do whatever you want to do, Ian," my father assured me.

But I wanted to be just like him. I was perfectly comfortable at the cemetery, and I admired the depth and the purpose that it gave to his life.

"Don't let it hold you back from other things."

So I didn't.

I took up the fiddle, I went to local schools like all the other boys my age, and I played some mediocre golf with my old man. I had plans to eventually enroll at university. At St. Andrews.

Already, I was intrigued by the challenges of landscaping and architectural design.

Especially cemeteries and golf courses, both links and parkland.

I also had boyish intentions to marry Heather MacDonald.

A bonnie young girl.

At school, I also did my bits of rugby. Which I greatly loved.

Then one day when I was twelve, the coach said:

"A big one like you might toss the caber."

Which I tried.

Then tried the hammer, which I liked even more.

At the age of sixteen, I was already two inches past six feet and unusually strong for my age. Surely my work at the graveyard didn't hurt.

My life was content.

Blessed.

It's true that I'd grown up a motherless boy. The love of my father's life had died after a sudden fever when I was four years old. So, unfortunately, I knew her not at all. I knew nothing but my life with my father, a remarkable man, on the cemetery grounds, and I never actually missed the mother I couldn't remember. My father would, of course, tell me lovely stories, and sometimes I'd see the other lads with their moms, and I'd think how wonderful it was. But I was never deeply affected by the loss I'd never felt.

My father made sure of that.

By the time of the Highland Games in Cowal, I was sixteen. I'd been training the hammer for four years, working hard on technique. I was already ready for the senior event, but I still had a year left in the juniors, and I was favored to win.

I was dressed, as I always dressed for competition: black "SKYE" t-shirt, dark blue-green MacDonald kilt, white knee socks, and my bladed black boots.

The truth is, by the time I was ready for my last throw, I'd already clinched the juniors with a toss of 132. So the last toss was a "vanity" toss. Mostly for the crowd.

For me.

When it was my turn, I looked over at the crowd, looking for my father. At his right was pretty Heather, dressed in jeans and a white windbreaker, at his left was a little family I'd heard about, but never encountered. The Kinnells. Visiting from America. Two handsome parents, as Scot as me and my dad, and in between the parents there was a gangly little lass with reddish honey hair, a MacDonald kilt that didn't fit quite right, probably purchased within the past few days, a dark green sweater, and a New York Yankees baseball cap.

She smiled, and my life was never the same.

But, of course, she was much too young. Much too young for the attractions I felt. The feelings I felt. So I pushed them aside.

But Heather noticed.

She noticed everything.

I stepped over, dug in, anchored myself in the turf. Then I took three decent winds over my head and released, tossing a sorry hammer.

I should have been embarrassed, but I didn't care, as the audience clapped politely. After all, despite the mis-toss, I'd already won the competition.

But I was distracted.

I looked over for the little girl, but she and her parents were gone. My father too.

Before the trophy presentation, I walked over to Heather.

I can still remember exactly what she said.

Exactly.

"Some dopey Scot just got himself smitten by a little Yankee girl."

I kidded her back.

What else could I do?

But in the back of my mind, which was confused and disordered, I was wondering if I'd ever get to see the little Yank again.

Later that evening, I went to meet my father at Strone Inn, and he was sitting at the far table with the

Kinnells. The parents. Needless to say, I was disappointed. They were finishing up their meal, and, as I got closer to the table, I noticed that the little girl was there as well. Asleep. Cuddled up next to her father, resting on his shoulder.

Once again, as earlier, I was thunderstruck.

It's the best word I've got.

I managed to say hello, and my father introduced me to the Kinnell parents. The father, Angus, had once sung Gaelic tunes with my father, and, as it turned out, they were old friends, growing up as neighbors on Skye.

But it was time to go.

They'd gotten bad news from the States and would have to cut short their vacation in Scotland.

Angus's brother-in-law, the husband of his sister Katie Kinnell MacDonald had died back home. An unanticipated heart attack.

"He's been a good one," Angus explained, "and my Katie's crushed."

The bill was paid, and the adults stood up. I was still standing in the aisle. Then Angus bent over and very carefully lifted his sleeping angel into his arms. Then we all walked outside to the parking lot.

To their rented car.

Angus looked at me.

"If you can win the hammer, Ian, then you can hold my precious lassie without a drop."

Then he handed me his bonnie little girl named

Polly.

He pulled out his keys and opened the back door of the SUV.

I looked at her face. Close to mine.

I'm a digger, Jimmy, not a writer, so I could never describe how I felt holding Polly Anna Kinnell in my arms.

Her father took hold of his sweetness once again and placed her carefully, like precious cargo, in the back seat of the red Cherokee.

"Thank you, Ian," he said.

I nearly thanked him.

"How old is she?" I asked.

"Thirteen at the moment."

"She's beautiful," I said stupidly.

"Well, let's not tell her," he laughed.

Then we said goodbyes, and they drove off, and I stood there with my father in the darkness.

"I could love that girl," I said.

"Maybe you should," he said.

Then he got the guilts.

"Would Heather mind?" he asked.

It seems that my father understood his son and bonnie Heather MacDonald better than we did. He told me years later that he wasn't at all surprised when we fell apart. Or that Heather went down to St. Margaret's.

"She's a remarkable lass, my boy. Your dearest dear friend. But she's on a higher plane."

I knew what he meant.

Heather did too.

So I won the toss, and my life moved on.

Two years later, I was off to St. Andrews, as Heather and I began drifting apart, and I got my internship with Foley Designs in Edinburgh. Then tragedy stuck. My father was killed in a car crash on the A835. No ice, no snow, no rain. Just a drugged-out moron in a pick-up. It hurt terribly, of course, but I'd been prepared my whole life for my father's death. By my father. By the work we did together. By our lives amid the dead.

As he would have wished, I refused to let it destroy my life, and I was rewarded with the odd ramification of another terrible tragedy. The death of James Michael MacBride, my father's younger brother, my beloved uncle, the father of my favorite cousin Jimmy MacBride.

In some inexplicable work-related accident.

Which brought Jimmy, the Memory Boy, my best friend, into my life full-time and made my life a wonder.

Wonderful.

We went off to St. Andrews together, then Edinburgh for a bit, then came back home to the cottage and the graves.

I was blessed. Content. But I still thought about that Yankee girl. All the time. Even though I knew it was foolish. A lingering fantasy of some kind about a young girl, now a young woman, who, as they say, didn't know me from Adam, who lived over 3000 miles away, off at some university, somewhere in New York City, with surely a thousand admirers.

Maybe even engaged.

Maybe even married.

The phone rang.

"It's Angus Kinnell," he explained.

His pretty Polly had been damaged in a serious car crash. *Very* serious.

"Can you come?"

He was a Scot from Brogaig at the north end of the island. He knew my father, and he knew about diggers, and he was desperate.

Was it a "sign" of some kind?

It might seem odd, given my own superstitions and dispositions, that I'm not that much for "signs."

But this one got me thinking otherwise.

I flew into some place called Newark, New Jersey, where Angus met me at the airport and drove me to the hospital.

I walked into the room, took her hand, and said a little prayer.

It's not much.

> *Dear Lord, I dig my life for you, please infuse dear [name] with your revitalizing spirit. Amen.*

You moved, then squirmed a bit.

I left the room and flew back to Scotland.

Angus felt it best that she shouldn't be told what happened, and I agreed.

She was twenty-one at the time, grown to a beautiful young woman, and I knew, having done what I'd done, that I should never see her again. *Never.* Because if I did, I'd probably fall in love with her (assuming I already hadn't), and a digger can *never* marry the one he's revived.

At any rate, it seemed that the 3,117 miles between us would be sufficient.

Then her mom passed, then Angus came back home.

He set up his little shop in Armadale, purchased a house nearby, and visited Jimmy and me all the time.

Fiddling.

Singing the Gaelic.

Talking of the old days with my father. Back when they barnstormed the Highlands, singing the old Celtic songs and fiddling the old Celtic tunes that never die.

Talking about his chocolates.

Talking about his Polly.

All of which I cherished. Even though, sometimes, it was difficult to hear about his daughter's romantic relationship with an Olympic athlete. A famous gold medal winner.

Including the possibility of an engagement.

But instead, a harsh rejection.

I considered flying to some place called

Milwaukee and kicking the shite out of the bastard.

But I didn't.

For four years, I'd been worrying that she'd come to Skye to visit her father. I even planned, in the back of my mind, that if she ever did come, I'd take Jimmy on a trip through the Western Isles.

Then, one afternoon, I could hear Angus playing with his fiddle over near Bonnie Jean's grave, as he did every Friday.

Then it stopped mid-tune, and I knew before I got there.

He was lying over his beloved's grave, dead from a dead heart.

Which damaged my own as well.

Which also meant that his beloved Polly Anna would finally be coming to Skye.

But I couldn't run. Angus was a dear dear friend, and it was up to me to place him in the soil. In consecrated ground. So I determined to keep myself, as much as possible, out of the way.

So Jimmy and I went to the viewing before it was opened to the public, and we sat in the far back of the church during the funeral. Poor Polly was obviously devastated, seemingly unaware of anything, least of all an obscure cemetery attendant and his young cousin.

Even at the burial, I kept my distance, but it seemed as though she saw me from a distance, and I didn't know what to make of it.

But it was all over.

I was safe.

Then out of nowhere, she showed up at the Sult, got loaded faster than any Scot I'd ever seen, and took her griefs out on me.

Fine.

I'm a big lad, and so is Jimmy.

The only benefit was meeting her ex-boy Matt Brooks, who turned out to be a highly decent chap. Whom, it seemed to me, might be good for Polly.

Or for *any* young woman.

So it was all over.

Once again.

Right?

But the next day, in the midst of a torrential, she knocked on my door, put on Jimmy's sweats, and kissed me before she left.

Why would she do such a thing?

Such a wonderful thing.

Who knows?

Why had I felt the way I'd felt the previous twelve years since those Highland Games?

Who can explain such things?

Certainly not me.

You know the rest.

We met at Lake Placid, and she did it again.

It almost seemed like she didn't know what she was doing.

Then I made the mistake of telling her that Jimmy and I were stopping in New York City.

You know the rest.

Greenwich Village, St. Anthony's Cemetery, and then the Village once again for Dion DiMucci.

My mind was a perfect mess, but I enjoyed every minute.

Simply being in her presence.

Then I escaped.

Jimmy and I got ourselves back to Skye, and I did my best to put it behind me. Then on Christmas Day, she was standing in front of my house in the snow.

You know the rest.

So I ask myself once again:

What have I done?

Are we destined to be happy?

Are we destined to be terribly sad?

34. Apartment

Friday, January 8th

Crack!

The pistol went off.

Rickie and her dad, still in his uniform, were sitting on the couch in the living room of our small apartment on 119th Street. Actually, it would be more accurate to say that Rickie was bouncing up and down on the edge of the couch in agitated anticipation. They were watching Matt's final 500 at the European Championships in Heerenveen in the Netherlands.

At the famous Thialf Speed Skating Arena.

I was standing right behind the couch, confident as always.

Matt was in the inner lane, matched with a powerful German, Kurt Klaussen, who was currently "top three" in the world.

They were off.

In a blur.

Rickie kept yelling, "Come on, come on, come

on!"

As the sports announcer on the television was saying things like:

"A strong start for both!"

"Brooks is making his move!"

"Both at record pace!"

Then it happened. Matt's left blade slipped a bit, and he instantly hit the ice and slid rapidly into a wooden barrier. It looked very violent.

"Brooks is out!

Rickie was stunned, completely drained.

"Damn," her dad said, summing things up nicely.

"Klaussen finishes with an excellent 33.86."

Rickie turned around.

"What happened?"

I wasn't sure.

"It looked like a cramp, Rickie. Maybe a pull. I hope that's all it is."

The camera focused on Matt, who was now surrounded by a crowd of medics and trainers. Poor Klaussen. He'd just won the European Championships, and he wasn't getting any attention.

Eventually, Matt stood up, and everyone at the arena applauded.

The announcer tried to clear things up.

"It seems to be a groin pull."

Rickie turned around again.

"What does *that* mean?"

I moved over to the chair facing the couch and sat

down.

"It means it'll hurt a lot, and he'll be out a few months, but it shouldn't be a problem in the long run. The Olympics are still two years away."

Rickie, like her father, was greatly relieved.

So was I.

Sgt. Moreno picked up the remote and muted the television.

"At least, it isn't serious," he decided.

"He'll be back," I assured them both.

But Rickie was now on another track.

"You know what *I* think?" she asked rhetorically.

"I can't wait," I said.

"I think his *real* injury is a broken heart."

She looked at me, the villain in the piece.

"I talked to Matt last week," I justified myself, "and he's doing just fine. As a matter of fact, he's been spending some time with that pretty skater-girl we met at Córdoba's."

"I liked her," Rickie remembered.

"Me too."

"But why," she lamented, "didn't he fall in love with me? He's pretty much perfect."

"What about my gravedigger?" I kidded back with mock indignation.

She rolled her Rickie eyes.

"Yeah, that one too. He seems too good to be true. Do you have any idea how lucky you are, Miss Polly?"

"Yes."

I meant it.

Satisfied, Rickie stood up and looked down at her old man.

"Another beer?"

"Sounds great."

Rickie vanished into the kitchen, and I took her place on the couch next to her father.

He was as close to a father as I had left in the world.

"When are you leaving?" he asked.

"A few weeks. I'll be living at my dad's place for a while, so we can get to know each other better. But I'll be back, and I expect you to come to Scotland and give me away."

"I wouldn't miss it."

I got even more serious. I'd always valued the man's opinions.

"Do you think we're rushing things too much?"

"Maybe. Maybe not. But not if you're *sure* he's the one."

"He's the one."

"Then be with each other as much as you possibly can. Life's too short for anything else."

"I will. I promise."

35. Doctor's Office

Monday, January 11th

"**Sorry, Polly, it's** been a long day!"

I was back in Scotch Plains, sitting in Jack Cooper's office. He was running behind schedule as usual, looking a bit harried, but pleasant as always.

He sat on the top of his desk and relaxed.

"Well, I've heard the marvelous news, Polly! Congratulations!"

"Thanks, Jack, I'm very excited, and I expect you to be at the wedding."

He liked the idea.

"I'll be there. It's the perfect excuse to go to Scotland."

Then he got more serious.

"Any progress with the taste buds?"

"Not really. Things still aren't right."

He thought it over.

"Is that why you're here?"

Maybe he was wondering if I was dissatisfied with

Dr. Prescott, but I wasn't.

I shook my head.

"No, Jack, I came here to do some matchmaking."

He laughed.

"I caught you eyeing my pal, Rickie, at Córdoba's that night, and I think you should take her out, fall in love, and get married."

He laughed again.

"Fine. It's settled."

"Well, that was easy. Here's her number."

I handed him one of his own office cards with Rickie's name and phone number written on the back.

He put the card in the pocket of his white medical coat and looked at me more seriously.

"Why are you *really* here, Polly?"

"I want to know the truth about my accident."

It clearly made him uneasy, so I tried to help.

"Ian told me to talk to you."

"Good," he said, relaxing. Then he stood up from the desk and sat down in a chair near my own.

I remembered a few things out loud.

"All I can remember is that I was driving home from the shore, and some drunken guy in an SUV sideswiped my car, and I woke up four days later. As if unharmed. Without a bruise or a scratch. Like that Bruce Willis character in the movie *Unbreakable*."

He smiled, as I remembered some more.

More details.

It was a summer Sunday afternoon, and I was

driving home from Manasquan, having spent the weekend with a childhood friend from Scotch Plains. I was cruising north on the Garden State, without a care in the world, thinking about Charlotte Brontë, because I had a test in my Victorian Lit class on the coming Tuesday, and I remember that I was thinking about *Villette*. How Lucy Snowe was pretty hard to relate to. Too cold. Too much "snow." So I was wondering, given the book's biographical origins, why Charlotte had done things the way she'd done them.

Suddenly, there was a tremendous crash behind me, over my left shoulder, into the back of my Charger SXT, and everything went black. Everything. I had no recollection of anything for the next four days. No skidding, no embankment, no final crash, no ambulance, no medics, no doctors, no nurses, no visitors, no nothing.

Just blackness.

Like a dreamless sleep.

Then I woke up like nothing had happened.

I opened my eyes, and Jack and my mother and my father were standing next to the bed, and I said, "What happened?" And my mother said, "How do you feel?" And I said, "I'm fine." And I sat up, and Jack checked me over, and I dressed myself and went home.

Alert, unmarked, and painless.

Two days later, I aced the make-up exam for my Victorian Lit class.

I looked at Jack.

"So what happened?"

"It was *really* bad, Polly. You were banged up something terrible, and you were completely unresponsive. Beyond hope. Then Angus showed up with this young guy he called 'Ian,' who was dressed in beat-down work clothes, work boots, and opaque black sunglasses. He walked into the room, took your hand, said some super-short prayer, and you stirred in the bed. Then Ian looked at Angus, and he left the room. As soon as he was gone, your eyes popped open and you wanted to go home."

"That's it?"

"That's it, Polly. I've seen a lot of strange stuff in my practice, but never anything like that. At the time, I wasn't much for the spiritual side of things, but that made me rethink myself."

He seemed amazed by his own memories, as if speaking to himself.

"I saw what I saw. The guy walked into the room, said a one-sentence prayer, and you came back to life."

What!

I was knocked back.

Stunned!

"I was dead?"

"Yes."

"Actually dead?"

"Yes."

"For how long?"

"Three days. When Ian arrived at the hospital, you

were down in the hospital morgue. On a slab. But I moved you back to a hospital room when Angus texted that his 'friend' was on the way."

"How did I die?"

"Massive head injuries. Your brains were smashed, Polly. Everything shut down, but your father begged me to wait, so I convinced the hospital to keep you in the cooler. I felt like a perfect idiot, but I did it anyway."

"Are you sure about this?"

"I'm positive."

36. Central Park

Monday, January 11th

I was sitting in the park again, near Rabbie Burns, thinking about death. Thinking about the supposed fact that I was some kind of walking dead. Some kind of Lazarus. Back from a void that I had no recollection of, no memory of, no awareness of.

It seemed so incredibly preposterous that I wondered if I should just shut it all down and forget about it. That I should act as if what Ian and Jack *thought* had happened, had never really happened.

On the other hand, whatever *did* happen certainly explained Ian's weirdo reluctance to act on his attractions for me and his fears about a possible relationship.

Fine.

Maybe I should just leave it at that and press on with my life.

But it was hard not to believe Jack.

Or Ian.

Even, it seems, my father and mother as well.

Had they all witnessed the dead coming back from the dead? Or, at least, something close to it?

I suppose I'll never really know.

I watched other people walking through the park, wandering around on the brisk January afternoon. Couples, solos, a few small groups, all full of life. With places to go, with things to do, even though death was waiting around the corner.

For all of us.

Who knows, maybe the reaper really did come for me back then.

Maybe I should just put it out of my mind.

He'll be coming back again anyway.

That's for sure.

But I wasn't feeling as grim as all this might sound. Actually, I was feeling grateful for the people who loved me back then. For the people who still loved me. I was feeling very grateful to be alive.

Whether or not I'd been dead once before.

I speed-dialed Scotland and listened to the message:

"This is Ian and Jimmy. We're sorry we missed you."

The beeper beeped, and I left a message for the one I loved.

"I'm sorry, too. I'm missing you, Ian. I talked to Jack Cooper this morning, and it's quite a lot to comprehend, but I'm doing my best. I certainly understand the concerns you've had, but I want you to know that I'm not worried. I'm not afraid. Not at all."

I paused.

Then continued.

"I love you, Ian, and even though it seems impossible, I love you even more than before. I'm certain, within my heart, that we're destined to be together forever. To be married forever. Goodnight, my love, and give my love to Jimmy."

I hung up and wondered where they were.

Evening shadows were creeping into the park. I looked at my watch. It was 5:02.

10:02 on Skye.

Then something came over me.

Something ugly.

Like a wave of painful unpleasantness. Something deeply distressing. Which immediately swept through my entirety like a vicious and violent wind.

Here one moment, then gone.

I felt terribly apprehensive.

Fearful.

My mother often told me that "second sight" ran in the family, which I always put in the same category as her wonderful ghost stories. But the Scots take such things seriously. They take our intimate connections with the ones we love *very* seriously. As if we're in touch all the time. Always. Even when far apart.

Had something happened to Rickie? Or Matt? Or Ian? Or Jimmy? Or any of the people I held closest in the world? Or was this horrible feeling, this deep uneasiness, simply the result of being told by a seemingly-rational medical doctor and close friend that I'd been raised from the dead seven years ago?

I had no idea.

I wondered if I should call Scotland again, which seemed a bit foolish, a bit alarmist.

So I didn't.

37. Apartment

Monday, January 11th

Three hours later, I was sitting on the couch, munching popcorn, and watching Jimmy's favorite movie with Rickie.

Just Like Heaven.

Mark Ruffalo was finally facing the fact that he now had a ghost in his new apartment. Who looked a lot like Reese Witherspoon.

My cell went off.

With an ugly ring.

Rickie paused the movie, and I answered.

It was Fr. Buchanan.

Ian and Jimmy had been in an accident.

I listened and tried not to panic.

My heart was slamming in my chest.

They were driving to Inverness, close to the hospital, when a lorry skidded on the ice and crashed into the ambulance. Flipping it twice.

"Twice?" I said.

Yes, the old priest explained. Twice. Jimmy's all right, but Ian was knocked unconscious. He's now in a room at St. Anthony's Hospital.

"Is it bad?"

"Yes."

"When did it happen?"

"Around ten o'clock."

When I was sitting in Central Park.

I thanked the priest, then explained to Rickie what I'd been told. I was definitely in shock, but I needed to keep moving.

Rickie understood.

"You pack, honey. I'll get you on the next flight."

Then she kissed me on the forehead.

What was going on with my life?

38. Inverness

Tuesday, January 12ᵗʰ

The decorations were gone.

Christmas was gone.

The whole hospital seemed like the morgue.

Despite my exhaustion from sleepless flights, I rushed down the hospital corridors into Ian's room.

Before I took off from Heathrow for Glasgow, I got in touch with Lachlan, and he met me at the airport. We drove north into the Highlands to Inverness. Maybe I should have tried to sleep in his taxi, but instead I told him everything.

My "death" seven years ago.

Ian's prayer.

The creepy feeling in Central Park.

Ian's accident.

He was, I realized, my new "confessor." Someone I could tell about all the idiocies of my life. About all the things that didn't make sense. About my feelings. About my fears.

About the terrors just below the surface.

There was a young nurse standing in Ian's dark room.

"I'll get the doctor."

She immediately left the room, probably glad that she didn't have to answer my questions.

Within the shadows, Ian was lying in his hospital bed. Connected to nightmarish plastic tubes and monitoring wires. There was a deep gash across his forehead, and his pallor was deathly.

I took his hand,

"Don't you leave me, love."

I was terrified.

I stood there for a timeless stretch of time until the doctor entered the room behind me.

"I'm Dr. MacAllister."

I turned around.

He was a competent-looking man in his late fifties.

"I won't be lying, Miss Kinnell."

He was Scots-honest.

Direct.

"He's in a crisis at the moment, and tonight's crucial."

"Will he live through the night?"

"I'm not certain if he will."

Maybe it was a good thing that I was sleepless and already benumbed.

He handed me a tissue, and I realized that tears were streaming down my face, but I wasn't about to give up.

"Where's Jimmy?" I asked rather desperately. "We need Jimmy! Right now!"

"The young boy?"

"Yes."

"He came through it fine, so I sent him home this afternoon. Since we've got an ice storm hitting tonight, he left with the priest from Skye."

"He wasn't injured?"

"No."

"Not at all?"

"No."

"Does that make sense?"

"Not really, but it's what happened."

He repeated himself.

"There's a big storm brewing, Miss Kinnell."

"I know."

I took out my cell and called Jimmy.

It rang three times, which seemed like forever, and I was terrified that he wouldn't answer.

He did.

"Jimmy and Ian."

"Jimmy?"

"Bonnie Miss Polly."

"Where are you, Jimmy?"

"Home."

I was more than relieved.

"Did you ever dig in the cemetery with Ian?"

"Tuesdays and Thursdays."

"Thank God. I'm coming tonight, Jimmy. Be brave!"

I hung up.

The doctor was still concerned.

"The weather's going nuts out there."

"Just keep him alive, doctor. I'll be back in a few hours."

I rushed out of the room, flying down the long white corridors.

39. Cottage

Tuesday, January 12th

Everything finally caught up with me, and
I conked out in the back of Lachlan's taxi.

The nothingness felt good.

Comforting.

Nothing but blackness.

"Almost there, lassie."

I stirred, sitting up in my seat.

It all came back. Like an avalanche. Like a
different kind of blackness.

I thought of my love.

Who might already be dead.

I pushed it from my mind and looked through the
taxi window.

"Snow," I said.

"Aye, a snowy icy hell."

I recognized where we were.

As planned, Lachlan was heading to Ian's cottage.
The taxi company wanted his cab back in Glasgow

before he got "iced under" in the Highlands. So before I'd fallen off to sleep, I asked him to go directly to Ian's cottage, where we could pick up Jimmy. Then Lachlan could drop us at my father's place in Armadale.

I knew that my dad's Equinox was still sitting in the driveway.

"You shouldn't be going back tonight," he said.

Meaning the hospital.

I was tempted to lie, but I didn't.

"I'll be safe, Lachlan," I promised. "Besides you still have to drive back to Glasgow yourself."

"Aye, but *away* from the storm."

"Don't worry, I'll be fine. I promise."

Then I settled back into the seat and fell instantly asleep, leaving all my problems behind, lurking in the conscious world.

But now I was awake again, trying not to panic, trying not to think too much, trying not to break down.

There was too much to do.

Outside the taxi's icing windows, within the lightly falling snow, was Tarskavaig Cemetery. Filled with the graves of the ones that Ian and his father and his grandfather had once buried. With respect. With love. Including my father and my mother. Including some who were unnamed, unwanted, unloved. Yet also treated with proper respect. Also buried with care in consecrated ground. Surely the souls of the dead would protect him tonight.

Surely.

Lachlan pulled his taxi in front of the cottage, where Jimmy was sitting on the front porch, bundled, with a thick wool cap, hooded parka, and a red scarf covering most of his face.

All I could see were his eyes.

It seemed as though he was waiting for me.

"There's the lad," Lachlan said, but I was staring at the snow-covered Land Rover sitting in front of the porch. Not a car I'd expect of a parish priest.

But why not?

Then the front door opened, and Matt came out.

A sight from the heavens. Huge, powerful, handsome, and dressed for the weather in black. But his right thigh was obviously heavily-bandaged beneath his pants, and he held an aluminum crutch under his left arm.

The Rover was obviously his rental.

He'd come to help.

I explained to Lachlan that I wouldn't need a ride to Armadale, and I thanked him for all his kindness, his sympathy, his fatherliness. Since I'd already paid my fares, including a preposterous tip, I got out of the taxi, and I heard him say:

"Where's my reward?"

His driver's side window had glided down a bit, and I walked over, leaned closer, and kissed him on the forehead.

"That's a lad who looks like he's good for keeping

you safe."

"He is."

He was relieved.

Then he drove off into the swirling snow.

Holding my travel bag, I stepped over to the porch.

Jimmy was oddly quiet. I suppose, like me, he was completely terrified. He'd lost his father eight years ago, and now his bestfriend/cousin/guardian was knocking on death's door a hundred miles away.

I went over and hugged him.

"Miss Polly," he said.

I looked at him directly.

"Do you know the digger's prayer?"

"Yes."

"Good."

I looked at Matt.

"I'm so glad you're here."

He knew I meant it.

"I came as soon as I heard."

Which was the "way" Matt was.

He smiled at himself.

"I was in such a rush that I even took my 'gear' bag."

"Well, we won't be needing your skates tonight, Matt, but we need to leave for Inverness right now."

He seemed unfazed.

"Fine."

That was that.

If anyone could handle the snow and the cold and

the ice, it was a guy who'd excelled his whole life at the winter games.

"I wish you weren't so crippled," I kidded, surprising myself.

Matt smiled.

"Still a better man than most," he kidded back.

Got that right.

40. Bridge

Tuesday, January 12th

I called the hospital from the road.

Ian was still alive.

We were approaching the bridge on A82 that led into Inverness. About eight miles from the hospital.

"We're almost there."

Matt just nodded, staring intently at the storm in front of him, which completely surrounded us.

I'd spoken too soon.

"Damn!"

The creeping traffic stopped.

Dead.

Matt had driven the whole trip from Skye. Carefully, steadily, through all the slow-downs, roadblocks, detours, and abandoned vehicles. There was probably more than two feet of snow out there, with ice underneath, and it was still coming down.

The temperature on the dash said -12C, which I knew was around ten degrees Fahrenheit.

When we left Ian's cottage, I naturally assumed that I'd be driving. It was perfectly clear, with every step, that Matt was in a great deal of pain. Groin injuries can bring down even the toughest athletes.

But Matt could see that I was pretty drowsy.

And dopey.

"Have you slept in the past twenty-four hours?"

I couldn't lie, so I told him the truth.

"I got about two hours in the back of Lachlan's taxi."

That settled it.

"I'm driving," he decided.

"You sure, Matt?"

"Yeah, I'm fine. It's four-wheel drive, but there's no clutch. I drove it all the way from Glasgow."

"In agony?"

"A bit," he admitted.

When we hit the approach to the bridge we'd been on the road for more than four hours to cover just a hundred miles. I could tell that Matty was in a lot of pain, but he never said a word.

Jimmy, sitting in the back, was eerily silent.

"How's he doing?" Matt asked, as we sat helpless in the line of stopped cars.

I took a look. Jimmy seemed catatonic. Almost. Maybe it was a kind of sleep. A kind of waking terror-sleep.

"How's my Jimmy?" I asked.

"Not good," he said.

"We'll be there soon," I promised.

But we were stuck.

Zero miles an hour.

I turned back to Matt.

"How was he before I came?"

"He was *very* spooked at the hospital, but the priest helped a lot. But when we got back to Skye, the priest had to rush off to a sick parishioner. Ever since then, Jimmy's been in a kind of weird 'waiting pattern.' Quiet and frightened."

"Ian's his whole world," I said, not knowing what else to say.

In the hazy headlights, we could see a bundled-up policeman slowly making his way from car to car, surely bringing bad news.

It was worse than I thought.

He tapped on the glass, and Matt lowered his window.

"I'm afraid you'll be turning things around. The bridge has iced itself, and we've shut it down."

I called across the front seat.

"We've got to get to the hospital! It's a matter of life and death."

He looked at me sympathetically.

"I'm sorry, young lass, but even if I let you attempt a crossing, there's a six-car pileup at the other end. The road's completely blocked off. No one's getting into Inverness tonight."

I was crushed, and he could see it, but he had

similar bad news to spread to all the other cars behind us.

He looked at Matt and pointed off to his right.

"You can turn around over there."

Then he moved along, to the car right behind us.

But Matt wasn't ready to give up yet. He pulled his Rover down a snowy embankment close to the edge of the river or loch or whatever it was. Where undulating snow with areas of exposed black ice extended to the other side. Nearby, a group of young boys were happily sledding down the embankment toward the edge of the ice.

I stared out at the night.

Helpless.

Seven miles from the one I loved.

Seven miles from the one I was determined to save, to resuscitate from the brink of death.

Matt had an idea.

Which sounded ridiculous.

"I know it sounds stupid, Polly, but I've got an old pair of skates in my gear bag in the backseat next to Jimmy."

I didn't understand.

"I could buy a sled from one of those kids and pull Jimmy across."

He knew that it was more important for Jimmy to get to the hospital than me.

I was incredulous.

"You can't skate, Matt. You can't even walk."

"I can make it across. It's only about 200 meters."

It looked a lot further than that to me. The far side looked like the end of the earth.

There was another problem.

"Is the ice solid enough?"

"Probably. But I'll check it out, Polly. If there's one thing I know about, it's ice."

I didn't argue.

He grabbed his bag from the backseat, pulled out an old pair of Vikings, and opened the driver's side door.

Immediately, a blast of wind/chill flashed through the car, but Matt was undaunted. Very quickly, he put on his skates then stood up in the snow.

Crashing right down.

In a terrible pain that even Matty couldn't ignore.

He looked at me from the ground.

"I'll be all right."

"No, you won't."

He knew it was true.

It was over.

For him.

"I can do it," I said.

He smiled.

It wasn't a smile of condescension. It was a smile of disbelief.

"You're the worst skater in North America."

"That's true. But I was taught by an Olympic gold medal winner, and I know how to put one skate in front of the other. I know how to keep myself upright."

He definitely didn't like the idea.

"These skates are a million sizes too big."

"We'll stuff some stuff inside," I said.

He shrugged and thought it over.

"I don't like it," he decided.

"I'm doing it," I decided.

That was that.

I looked back at Jimmy.

"Can we do it, Jimmy?"

"Yes."

"You sure?"

"I want my Ian."

He was ready for anything.

It was perfectly foolhardy, of course, and maybe I had no right to involve Jimmy, but Jimmy was the key to everything. I was fully prepared to risk my life for Ian, and so was Jimmy.

Twenty minutes later, we were down at the ice.

Matt, struggling with his crutch in the snow, had convinced one of the kids to "lend" him a sled for fifty pounds sterling and an autograph. I think the kids just wanted to see if I could make it. They were now watching from the embankment, probably discussing my negligible chances.

Matt finished adjusting my skates, and Jimmy was already sitting on the little wooden sled.

Ready and waiting.

Stoic and brave.

"How's the ice?" I asked.

"Fine, except for some open water near the bridge. Keep your distance, Polly."

"I will."

I was ready to go.

I stood up, a bit unsteady, like a newborn colt, but I caught my balance.

"I don't like it," he repeated.

I ignored him, took the rope to Jimmy's sled, and gradually made my way, warily, to the edge of the ice.

I looked back.

"You're a blessing, Matt Brooks."

He smiled.

"Ian's a lucky man."

I turned around and looked ahead.

Across the ice.

The wind was constantly shifting the falling snows. In some places, the ice was actually visible, black and windswept. In other places, there were high drifts, as high as three or four feet. Everywhere there was whirling snow. The hard sleety kind. Within shifting mists. It was quite forbidding, to say the least, but I could see a path to the other side. Surely I could pull a little sled across the open ice.

But Matty was worried, and he warned me.

"Don't let the winds blow you off course."

I nodded, then slowly, I moved forward a little bit, as Jimmy and his sled glided along behind me, gliding easily across the slick ice.

But Matt wasn't ready to give up yet, and I felt sorry for him. He wanted to try and walk across the ice with us. With his stupid crutch.

"Don't be an idiot," I said, as he tied my shoelaces together then looped my shoes around the back of Jimmy's neck and over his shoulders.

"Look who's talking," he said.

He was right.

Who was the bigger idiot?

I thought of a way to put an end to it.

"I don't want to have to worry about you, too."

He thought it over and agreed.

Saying nothing.

Now I was on my own.

Moving forward.

Initially, my progress was steady. I seemed almost unaware of the cold except for occasional frigid gusts of wind that seemed to burn at the surface of my eyes. Sometimes the whirling snow was blinding, and I'd stop, close my eyes, and wait for the burn to subside. Then I'd turn around and check on Jimmy, who was covered with a light dusting of snow, seemingly inanimate. It was pointless to try and communicate in the wind, so I simply nodded my head, and Jimmy nodded back.

Then I'd turn around, moving us forward again.

Weaving my way across the open black ice.

Away from the high mounds of snow.

Off to my right, I could see the soft lights on the

bridge and the stationary headlights of all the cars entangled at the other side. Hopefully, since everyone was driving so carefully tonight, no one was seriously hurt.

Ahead, across the water, across the ice, there were a few hazy lights at some distant homes lost in the overall whiteness.

Then my feet went numb.

Matt had done his best to pad his oversized skates with multiple layers of socks, but I wasn't used to this kind of cold and the numbness scared me.

About halfway across, the wind picked up.

Visibility was greatly diminished, and I could feel myself drifting to the right. Blasted by the wind. In the direction of the bridge. I did my best to fight against it, stopping several times to try and get my bearings, but nothing helped. I was pretty much snowblind, pressing forward on instinct, trying to avoid the bridge lights off to my right.

About fifty yards from the other side, I heard a crack. A tremendous crack. It ripped right through me like it ripped through the ice. It cracked my heart, and it cracked any confidence that I still had within my heart. I stopped where I was, waiting for a break in the swirling freezing winds. I'd drifted much too close to the bridge where the ice was less secure, where Matt had warned that there was open water.

Open death.

I turned around and Jimmy's sled was slowly

sinking into the freezing water. I was horrified. He sat right where he was, immobile and terrified, looking down into the dark waters flooding around the runners of his sled.

I assumed that we would die together.

I should have said a prayer of some kind.

Maybe I did.

"Daddy help me," I said in the back of my mind.

I dropped the rope, fell to my knees in the ever-seeping black water, and reached back for Jimmy's hand. He understood and put out his hand. I grabbed him tightly and pulled him with all my might, pulling him right off his sled, into the freezing slush surrounding him, pulling him toward me.

I was now lying flat on my stomach in the icy water, and I was gradually sliding toward Jimmy on the slick ice below. It seemed as though I would never have either the strength or the leverage to do what I needed to do, so I smashed the blades of my skates into the ice behind me. To brace myself. Then I pulled with all my might, looking the entire time into Jimmy's frightened eyes.

What did Ian once say?

"He can get scared sometimes. Really scared."

I was now looking right at it, fully expecting that the two of us would soon sink into the blackness.

Into death.

Behind Jimmy, I could see his sled sinking into the water.

It was gone.

I pulled harder.

Suddenly, Jimmy slid toward me, gliding on the ice, through the black water. Somehow, I managed to thrust us away from the pooling water, still on our stomachs, and we were able to crawl across the ice to the shore.

To safely.

I sat up and looked back across the ice. I couldn't see Matt. I was grateful that he hadn't seen what had just happened.

Jimmy sat up.

We were both hypothermic. Wet and shivering uncontrollably.

Somehow I managed to pull the skates off my completely numb feet, but I couldn't get my shoes on, and we didn't have any time to waste. I stood up in my layered soaked socks, got Jimmy to his feet, and we fought through the wind and the snow to the nearest house, which, fortunately, was close to the shore.

I felt like Scott of the Antarctic, but still alive, and so was Jimmy.

41. Arctic Cat

Tuesday, January 12th

The old man opened the door as soon as I knocked.

A *very* old man.

"Do you have a snowmobile?" I asked, stupidly.

He ignored me.

Immediately, he directed us both, me and Jimmy, to the couch in front of a welcome fire. Then he brought us warm clothes. I quickly changed in one of the bedrooms, and the old man helped Jimmy change in the living room.

My cell had survived, so I called the hospital.

Ian was still alive.

Then Jimmy and I sat in front of the fireplace until my feet came back to life. They hurt like hell, as they slowly revived themselves, but soon enough, I was ready to go.

The old man, Neill Purcell, was a teacher, a professor, and a widower, and well past retirement.

Most of his life, he'd taught chemistry at Inverness's University of the Highlands. These days he mostly watched rugby on the telly and thought pleasant thoughts about his dead wife.

"You'll need to be spending the night," he said, as if it was obvious.

Prof. Purcell was probably the nicest man on the planet, but *nothing* was keeping me from the hospital tonight.

Nothing.

I gave him a brief summary of my preposterous situation, wondering how an old academic, a "hard" scientist, would react to something like a "digger's prayer." But he didn't bat an eye.

What concerned him was the weather.

"It's much too nasty."

I insisted.

Within a half-hour of our knock on the door, Jimmy and I were sitting on Neill's Arctic Cat, getting final instructions. We were bundled, as warm as possible, in the clothes he'd given us, and I was anxious to get going.

I'd driven these snow-things before. With Matty, of course.

The professor looked down at Jimmy.

"All dry, little man?"

Jimmy nodded, sitting right behind me with his arms wrapped around my waist. Holding on for dear life.

But his fears were gone.

What did Ian say?

"He can get scared sometimes. Really scared. Fortunately, he gets over it quickly."

Neill pointed into the night, toward Inverness, over the shifting shadowy mounds of snow.

"It's about six miles once you cross the golf course."

I thanked him again, then again, then we took off.

Into the swirling winds, the swirling snow, the white mist.

42. Hospital

Tuesday, January 12th

We made it.

I parked the Cat at the front door, and we made our way down the endless dark corridors. It was late at night, almost midnight, but Dr. MacAllister was still on call, and he'd agreed to meet me at Ian's room.

He was clearly skeptical of my intentions, but he was also very understanding, willing to "put up" with me.

Despite my overall exhaustion, I wished I could pick Jimmy up and rush him to Ian's room. But I did my best to be patient, walking along beside him, slowly but steadily.

The halls were quiet, the visitors were long gone, and only a few nurses were seen here and there.

Finally, we entered the shadowed room.

It was exactly like before.

Ian, with his ugly tubes and wires, was lying with his eyes closed in a kind of sleeping death.

The doctor stood at his bedside.

"I don't see how you made it to Skye and back again."

He was very impressed.

"It was a miracle," I admitted, "and now we need another one. Has anything changed?"

"Nothing. No better, no worse."

I nodded, then looked at Jimmy.

He was terrified by the sight of Ian still lying helpless on the bed in front of him.

"You need to be brave, Jimmy."

He nodded.

"Do you know what to do?"

He shrugged.

"Take Ian's hand," I said, "and say the prayer."

He took Ian's hand.

I could see the tears welling in his soft blue eyes.

"Pray hard, Jimmy."

He concentrated, then said the little prayer in his little boy's voice, slightly wavering.

Dear Lord, I dig my life for you, please infuse dear Ian MacIan with your revitalizing spirit. Amen.

It was over.

It was done.

Nothing happened.

No movement of any kind.

The blackness tried to overwhelm me, but I fought against it.

"Try it again, Jimmy."

He did.

Dear Lord, I dig my life for you, please infuse dear Ian MacIan with your revitalizing spirit. Amen.

Nothing.

My resistance was gone.

I collapsed to the floor.

Everything went black.

43. Chapel

Tuesday, January 12th

When I revived on the floor of Ian's room, Dr. MacAllister was kneeling over me, checking me out.

"You need sleep, young lady, and you need it badly. I'll have the nurses set up cots in the room so you can spend the night."

I wasn't about to argue with his kindness.

He knew that my problems went far beyond sleeplessness. Even though the doctor had been naturally skeptical about the possible efficacy of Jimmy's prayer, he'd shown great compassion for the both of us. He was familiar, of course, with the desperations of his patients' families and friends, and he definitely admired the extremes that Jimmy and I had undertaken.

"You did everything you could," he said softly.

Which I appreciated.

But I wasn't convinced.

Had I *really* done 'everything' I could?

For an hour or so, Jimmy and I sat on our little cots. I was "beyond" sleep, and Jimmy was incapable.

We sat in the silence, close to Ian, until Jimmy spoke.

"I like the chapel."

All right.

Why not?

So we went to the chapel.

I could see why Jimmy liked the place. It was old-fashioned, with large religious murals, striking wooden statues, and lovely stained glass.

It was quiet and peaceful and comforting.

Jimmy and I sat in the chairs near the front.

We were all alone. The Memory Boy and his Chocolate Princess.

He stared intently at the main mural, and I did as well.

It portrayed a bearded old man, dressed like a hermit, kneeling in the dirt, amid the rocks, in front of a desert cave. Nearby, on the ground, there was a skull.

There was also a shovel stuck upright in the dirt.

Maybe I was too tired to be astonished, but I was.

I turned to Jimmy.

"Who's that?"

"St. Anthony"

I was confused.

"Anthony of Padua?"

"Anthony of Egypt."

He looked at me and clarified.

"My favorite."

I wondered why.

"Why?"

"He's the patron of gravediggers."

Then something came over me.

A kind of "understanding."

I stood up and looked at the old saint, whom I knew nothing about. An old bearded man in worn-out brown hermit robes, probably an ascetic, probably an anchorite.

Had I misunderstood the mysticism surrounding the concept of the digger? The superstition? The level of commitment?

I looked intently at St. Anthony.

"I think I understand," I said to the mural.

It was up to *me*, not Jimmy.

In the back of my mind, I made a determination. A promise to myself. Yes, let's even call it a vow.

For some reason, "Monday, Wednesday, and Friday" popped into my mind, and I didn't even think about it. I acquiesced.

Instantly.

It was over.

I sat back down, next to Jimmy, and pulled out my cell, glancing up at the saint again.

"Forgive me for using this thing in here."

He said nothing.

I checked the weather in Westchester county.

New York.

Forty-one degrees.

It sounded balmy.

I put away my cell and turned to Jimmy.

"Can you be brave, Jimmy?"

"I want Ian."

"I know. So do I. But we need to be brave, Jimmy. I'm not giving up. I promise."

He nodded.

"I need to go away for a while. Will you be brave, Jimmy? Matt can stay with you for a week or so, then Fr. Buchanan will take care of you until I get back."

He said nothing.

"I'll be back for you, Jimmy. I promise. I'll be back for Ian too. Don't be discouraged, no matter what happens. Can you do that? Can you be brave?"

"Yes."

"I'll be back," I repeated.

"Yes."

44. St Anthony's

Thursday, January 14th

I slept on the red-eye.

Finally.

From Heathrow to JFK.

Before I did so, I checked out the saint. The patron of the gravediggers.

St. Anthony of Egypt.

Who's *way* back there, born in the Third Century.

He was apparently raised in a prosperous family in some place called Comus in Egypt. When he was a young man, a few months after his parents died, he heard a reading of Matthew 19:21, and he immediately gave away all his wealth. He went into the desert, near a graveyard, and lived an ascetic life. It was a very long and charitable life, in which he served as a model for many others, often considered the "father" of the monastic life. He was imprisoned during the persecutions of Maximinus Daza, refuted the Arians, built at least one monastery, and died in the middle of the Fourth Century at the age of 105.

I fell asleep.

It was now two days later, two days since I'd stared at the mural of St. Anthony in Jimmy's little chapel. Now I was sitting in Mr. Palmer's office in Westchester waiting for Luis's lunch break. Eventually, the old man came into the room with his little lunch bag. He was dressed in his work clothes, which were worn and dirty, and he was very concerned.

"Is it Ian?" he said in his soft pleasing accent, which I would later learn was Argentine.

"How do you know, Luis?"

"I sense things sometimes. Vague things."

"Do you have the 'gift'?"

"No."

He was very clear about that.

When he sat down, I told him everything. Even the parts I had trouble believing myself.

He listened quietly.

"Do you know why I'm here, Luis?"

"I believe I do."

"Do you remember what you said to me back in December?"

"Yes."

I said it anyway.

"I will be at your service."

Which, at the time, seemed like a very odd way to phrase a lovely sentiment.

He nodded.

"Did you know that I'd be coming?"

He shrugged.

"I sense things sometimes," he repeated. "But always vague."

I was beginning to understand.

"Will you teach me, Luis?"

"Yes."

But he had a rather obvious concern.

"It's *very* hard work, niña."

"I know."

He had another concern.

"And it might not provide you with what you want it to provide you."

"I know, Luis, but I need to try."

He understood, and he nodded.

Then I explained the rest of it.

That Mr. Palmer had agreed to hire me as an "intern," to avoid potential union problems, that I'd need a list of appropriate work clothes, and that I was planning to rent a small apartment nearby.

I didn't want to commute from the city.

I also didn't want distractions.

"You'll stay with us," he said.

Which caught me off-guard.

"I couldn't do that, Luis."

"We'd be happy to have you."

He refused to take no for an answer.

The "we" he spoke of included his sister, Maria. I'd learn, soon enough, that his wife Carmelita had died a few years ago and his unmarried sister had moved in with him fairly recently. His two sons were now grown, out on their own, one married in Albany, one engaged in Philadelphia. Luis and Maria lived in Irvington, four miles from the cemetery, in a lovely little brick house.

When we were done, Luis stood up.

His lunch was unopened.

He handed me a list of clothes that I'd need for tomorrow morning. At five a.m.! I'd never thought about the obvious before, but burials, in most cases, take place in the morning, and Luis always left for work at five a.m.

At the bottom of the list was his address in Irvington.

"I'll call Maria, and she'll be waiting for you. When I get home this evening, we'll go to the trading station and get some clothes. Then you'll need to get to bed. Early."

I was ready.

Grateful.

I stood up and gave the old man a hug. I didn't want to cry, and I didn't. I just went soft. He knew all the desperations in my heart.

"You need to be brave, Miss Polly."

When he left the room, it felt especially lonely, so I pulled out my cell. It was time to listen to the message I'd been avoiding.

Ricky.

She was worried, frantic.

"Where are you, Polly! This isn't like you! I'm *very* worried. Matt says that you flew back to JFK, so where the hell are you! If you don't call me tonight, I'm having my dad get the cops moving on a missing persons."

There was a pause.

"I've also figured out the donor thing. Call me! Now!"

I did.

"It's me," I said stupidly.

"Thank God!"

She didn't know whether to be relieved or angry.

Anger won out, and I took a well-deserved tongue-lashing. In silence. When she'd expiated all her demons, I apologized and told her what I was doing.

"That's ridiculous, Polly!"

I couldn't argue.

"It's all I've got left."

"What about Jimmy?"

She was right, of course. It did seem strange that I wasn't sitting at the bedside of the one I loved, holding his hand, and comforting Jimmy.

"He undertands."

"Understands what?"

"What I'm trying to do."

She thought it over.

"You're a pair of idiots."

Then I told her about Luis, explaining that I'd be "out of the picture" for a while, but that I'd call her every Sunday afternoon to check in. I made it clear that I didn't want any surprise visits.

"It's total immersion."

For some reason, she didn't argue.

She was thinking about something else.

"Should *I* be heading to Inverness?"

"Not now, Ricky. There's nothing you can do there. Let's wait."

She understood.

There wasn't much a kindergarten teacher in Manhattan could do for a young man in a coma. Unconscious. With brain damage.

There was silence on the phone.

Fortunately, Rickie was never big on silence.

"I figured out the money, Polly. Actually, my dad did."

Two years ago, when I first started sending her money for the school, I thought it was a good idea to do it anonymously. So she wouldn't be able to refuse it.

Maybe it was a bad idea.

"I had more money than I needed," I said, which didn't explain the anonymity.

She didn't press it.

"I love you, Polly."

"I love you, Rickie."

"Do what you have to do, but don't have unrealistic hopes."

"I won't," I lied.

That was that.

She had to get back to her kids, her "brats," so we hung up together.

It was time to get to work.

45. Unclaimed

Thursday, January 21ˢᵗ

I've never done much manual work in my life.

After all, I tasted chocolate for a living.

Now I was getting pretty competent with a pick, decent with a shovel, and I'd learned how to operate pulleys, backhoes, and all kinds of other hydraulic equipment. I'd only been "at it" a week, but all my horrendous blisters had healed, and my aching muscles had stopped crying out in agony, and I was used to getting six hours of sleep, rising with the morning sun.

I was also getting comfortable with work clothes. With baggy clothes, leather gloves, and clunky work boots. I was also getting acclimated to the powerful smells of the soils in which I worked all day long, then brought home on my clothes every night, then washed away in my nightly shower.

I've never appreciated a warm shower so much.

I use the word "home" since Luis and Maria made it feel that way. He was always kind, an ever-patient mentor, and Maria was an angel. At fifty-eight, she was a few years younger than Luis, and she reminded me of my mother, which is always the highest possible compliment.

At work, at the cemetery, Mr. Palmer was worried about me all the time, especially in the beginning, and he was still checking on me every day, always during my afternoon break, when I sat on the same white bench where I'd sat last December with Ian, staring at the distant Hudson, trying not to wonder if I was out of my mind.

The "boys," as Luis called Carlos and Fernando, were also helpful, always hard-working, and always having fun with their work. Yet *always* respectful of the dead. Of their chosen vocation.

Fernando, like the diggers in *Hamlet*, was fond of stupid graveyard jokes, some of which I think Luis could have done without.

Carlos and I always laughed. Sometimes I traded chocolate jokes for Fernando's "graver" jokes.

Some of his stupidest were:

Where's the cemetery?
The dead center of town.

What time does a gravedigger start work?
The graveyard shift.

Why's the cemetery so popular?
Everyone's dying to get in.

How many dead people in that huge cemetery?
All of them.

I told you they were stupid!
But I did have a favorite:

The gravedigger texted his ex-girlfriend:
Wish you were here.

Luis wasn't averse to having some fun with all the serious work, but he always reminded us:

"Remember, gravediggers perform the final act of kindness for those in our care."

As it turned out, Luis, who'd never finished high school growing up in La Plata, not far from Buenos Aires, who'd learned English at night at a local adult learning program when he was seventeen, was quite a reader. His bookshelves were full of Borges, Dickens, and his favorite, Shakespeare.

Needless to say, *Hamlet* was his most favorite, specifically Act 5, Scene I, with the garrulous and witty gravedigger, who assures his co-worker:

There is no ancient gentleman but gard'ners,
ditchers, and gravemakers.

Sometimes, on break, Luis would recite Hamlet's Yorick lines, or sing one of the gravedigger's songs:

A pickax and a spade, a spade,
For and a shrouding sheet;
O, a pit of clay for to be made
For such a guest is meet.

Earlier today, Mr. Palmer came up behind my bench, now known as "Polly's Bench."

It was mid-afternoon.

Beginning as he always did.

"Any word?"

Meaning any word about Ian.

He knew that I began my break every day with a quick phone call to Jimmy, who was now at the rectory with Fr. Buchanan. The old priest had finally forced Matty to go back home, saying something like:

"This could go on for a long time, Matthew, and you need to get on with your own life. Jimmy's fine here with me, and we'll run up to Inverness several times a week."

Something like that.

Over and over, until Matty finally gave in.

"He's stubborn in his goodness," the old priest explained to me on the phone.

"Yes."

I looked up at Nicholas Palmer.

"Still the same."

We talked about my improving physical condition. My training. The dead.

I was grateful to be working with Luis and his team when they'd buried several of the dead this past week. But I wanted to bury someone myself. An "unclaimed." One I could bury all alone with just a pick and shovel. Some poor lost person whom I could lay to rest.

Luis approved of the idea, but he didn't think I was ready yet.

Neither did Mr. Palmer.

"We don't get too many up here, Polly. Maybe one or two each month, but I'll keep my eyes open."

"Thank you."

"Besides, the weather's a factor."

For a shovel-dig.

I nodded.

Fortunately, the weather had been unseasonably mild, but it wouldn't last.

It was finally time for Mr. Palmer to get back to the business of the dead.

"You know where I am if you need me, Polly."

I nodded again, gratefully.

Then he left me alone with all my thoughts, all my memories, all my altered ambitions, all my hopeful possibilities, all my fantasies.

46. St Anthony's

Sunday, February 14th

I sensed a shadow high above me, and I knew who it was as soon as I saw it.

Yes, I'd told him *not* to come, of course, that it wasn't necessary, but he'd always ignore me and say, "We'll see, young lass." Which meant that he'd probably be coming anyway. Eventually. I think he was worried that I might collapse. That I might not be able to make the trip back to Scotland by myself.

Without his help.

I was standing down in the grave I'd dug by myself. Three feet by eight feet, and five feet deep.

It was early in the morning, damp yet not too cold, exactly a month since I'd made my commitment to a mural of an ancient saint in a hospital chapel, and I was finally burying my first unclaimed.

My first unwanted.

They found the poor man near the Tappan Zee, maybe seventy years old, looking much older, surely a drinker, definitely alone.

Without identification.

"I've found one," Mr. Palmer said last Thursday.

So I decided to call him "John," and I spoke to him frequently as I was working. He was now in a donated coffin at the edge of the grave.

I looked up and saw the old priest who'd come all the way from Skye to tell me in person.

Who was older than "John."

Much older.

"Is he gone?" I asked.

It was a foolish question, but it had to be asked. Why else would the old priest have come this far?

"Yes."

I'm not really the fragile flower this story might make it seem. I've only collapsed once in my life, in Ian's hospital room, and that was simply a kind of "giving out." Everything had overwhelmed me at once. The grief, the sleeplessness, the helplessness, and the failure. I went black, as if someone had pulled the plug.

Now it was different.

My legs failed me. They grew oddly weak, and I could no longer support myself. I slumped back against the muddy side of the grave, sinking down to the cold dirt floor.

To my knees.

"Do I need to be coming down there?" the old man asked.

"No."

I quickly regained my strength, stood up, and climbed the little ladder, carrying my shovel.

I looked at John's coffin.

"I'd like to bury this one first."

"Fine. I'll say a few prayers."

I called Luis and the boys, who came immediately. Carefully, we lowered the coffin into the grave.

Manually. Steadily. No hydraulics.

Things went smoothly.

After the prayers, I tossed in the first shovel of dirt.

"We'll finish things, Polly," Luis said.

I nodded.

"Our flight's in two hours," the old priest said.

Luis and the boys knew what had happened. They knew that I was leaving, and they knew what I was hoping, but they said nothing about it.

I jammed my shovel into the dirt, then I hugged Luis like I used to hug my father.

"*Via con Dios*," he whispered.

Then I hugged Carlos, then Fernando.

There were no jokes today.

Then I left the grounds with the old priest at my side.

47. Ferry

Sunday, February 14th

"Can't this thing go faster?"

I was standing at the front rail of the ferry from Mallaig to Skye, staring into the black night, looking for Armadale.

The old priest stood next to me.

Indestructible.

Who'd flown from Scotland to New York, then back again, sleeping a bit on the planes.

"I've already spoken with the captain," he said, and I wasn't sure if he was kidding or not. Besides, it's just a half-hour crossing. At Armadale, I could drive my waiting rental straight to the rectory, pick up Jimmy, then head to Inverness.

For who knows what.

"Am I being a fool?"

"Good works are never foolish."

Which really didn't answer the question.

The love of my life had died last night. It was quite

simple. He'd flat-lined. They tried to revive him several times, and his death was called at 11:58.

Almost midnight.

I was glad that Jimmy wasn't there.

"Are you prepared for failure, lassie?"

It was a good question.

I'd spent the past month doing what I thought I *should* do, trying to remind myself that it might not work. That, yes, the digging might be efficacious in certain ways, but not necessarily the one that was most important.

Was I prepared?

"No, I'm not fully prepared, Father, but I'm trying to prepare myself to accept whatever will happen."

"Even should it be nothing?"

"Even should it be nothing," I repeated.

"At the very least, you and the boy can say goodbye."

"Yes."

What a horrible thought.

48. Inverness

Sunday, February 14th

"I'm not comfortable with this."

It was something he felt obligated to say, but he didn't press it. Despite the late hour, Dr. MacAllister met me at the front entrance of the hospital, then escorted the three of us to the morgue.

"I know," I said.

Jimmy said nothing. He definitely knew what was happening, but he was in a state of silent suspension.

Ian was dead.

His Ian.

It would be hard to see.

Inside the morgue, the attendant was ready. Ian was lying on one of the metal tables, covered with a sheet.

Just like the unwanteds, just like the unclaimed.

"Oh," Jimmy said softly, so I put my arm around him.

Death had given my love a deathly gray pallor. It

seemed as though he was gone forever. As if there was nothing left of him. Nothing at all.

Just death.

I faltered.

Everyone waited.

"Make your beseechment, my dear," the old priest said softly.

I let go of Jimmy, stepping closer to the metal slab. Then I took Ian's dead cold hand with my left hand, and I placed my right on his chest.

Dear Lord, I dig my life for you, please infuse dear Ian with your revitalizing spirit. Amen.

Nothing.

I was desperate.

Defeated.

"Reiterate yourself."

It was the old priest again.

I reaffirmed what I'd said in my heart a month ago, standing in front of the painted mural of St. Anthony.

"I promise that every Monday, Wednesday, and Friday, I'll dig with my husband."

Nothing.

More nothing.

I looked at Jimmy. He seemed catatonic.

I put my arm around him again. Somehow, I was determined to help him survive.

He looked at me.

Alert.

"Kiss him."

As odd as it seemed, maybe it wasn't so odd.

"Just like *Just Like Heaven*."

In the midst of all my exhaustions and griefs and disappointments, I smiled at myself.

Of course. That's why Jimmy liked *that* rom-com best of all. Not because of the ghost, because of the kiss.

I leaned over and kissed Ian on the mouth.

He was cold and dead.

Nothing happened.

So much for rom-coms and Disney movies.

Now it was time to be brave for Jimmy.

Ian moved.

The color was back in his face. He opened his eyes.

As if aware.

"Did Polly kiss me again?"

He looked at me directly.

"Has someone been digging graves?"

49. Kiss III

Sunday, February 14th

[Remembrance of Ian MacIan:]

She did it again.

Unexpectedly as always.

After all, I was dead this time.

Happening, of all days, on Valentine's Day!

So what's it like to be once-dead?

To be, like my fiancée, a member of the walking dead? Actually, it's not very different at all. It was like going to sleep, a dark dreamless sleep, then waking up. Under the most lovely of circumstances. Looking at the face of my love. With her lips on mine.

Yes, I realize that the morgue isn't exactly the most "lovely" of circumstances, but you can't have everything.

So what's it like to be dead?

Well, the oddest thing about "coming back" was that I *knew* stuff that I shouldn't know. This didn't happen to Polly seven years ago in her New Jersey hospital, but it happened to me in Inverness. Maybe it's because I've been a digger all my life.

That's the best guess I've got.

Anyway, I *knew* stuff when I revived. I knew that she'd been digging. I knew that she'd made some kind of vow. I knew that she'd done everything to try and bring me back. I didn't have any specific "images" in my mind of Polly digging away in the cold, sometimes for eighteen hours a day, in St. Anthony's Cemetery in Westchester. But I *did* know, somehow, that Carlos had been helping her, and that Jimmy had supported her. As had Fr. Buchanan.

I also knew that Jimmy had been brave.

That he'd been patient in his heart, that he'd done his best to deal with things, and I was proud of him.

Very proud.

Just like I always was.

So back to the original question.

What's it like to be dead?

To be some kind of Lazarus?

Well, in my case, it certainly gives one a renewed appreciation for life.

For the fact that life is precious.

I remember my father saying one time, "It's because life is so precious that death is precious as well."

Which might seem a bit peculiar, but I think that he meant that if we have a respect for life, then we should also respect its final resolution. It's earthly termination. Whatever might or might not come after death, we should always recognize the life of the dead with a proper denouement.

With proper respect.

"Into that good night."

Now, more than ever, I was resolved to live my life preciously, to love lovingly, to take care of the dead respectfully.

Above all, to love my Polly.

Above all, to love my Jimmy.

"For once I was lost, then I was found."

50. Armadale Castle

Saturday, December 25th

Ian was at his fiddle.
Singing along with himself.
A true Gaelic voice.
A melodic baritone.

Bidh mo ghaol-sa dhi buan am feasda
Air Eilean àluinn a' Cheò.

Which, as I attempted to translate at the beginning of this story, means something like

I will love my love forever and ever
On the beautiful Island of Skye.

The song, "*Mo Rùn Gàidhealach,*" meaning "My Highland Love," is the one that my father composed for my mother over thirty years ago. Which he was singing when he died at her grave over Tarskavaig cliffs.

It was Ian's wedding present to his new wife.

(Me.)

After what Jimmy (you) likes to call the "revival" kiss at the Inverness morgue on Valentine's Day, we had ten months to prepare for our Christmas wedding.

Ian, instantly revived, sat up on the metal slab. The nurses found the same clothes he'd been wearing when he was admitted after the accident, and, within thirty minutes, the four of us were on the road heading home to Skye, with Jimmy and Fr. Buchanan sitting in the backseat.

Ian, as impossible as it seems, had no physical repercussions from the accident, as well as no awareness of the month he'd spent in a coma.

Or dead.

But I'd like to go back to that kiss again. I hope you're not getting tired of hearing about it, but there was yet another peculiar repercussion. Not as dramatic as coming back from the dead, but still extremely significant to me.

The aftertaste.

The aftertaste of Ian McIan.

Yet something even more than that, something lingering.

Somewhere on A82, I decided to check it out.

"We need to make a stop."

I pulled my rental, a Ford Explorer, into the first gas station I could find. As Ian topped off the tank, I went inside and brought a Cadbury "dairy milk" chocolate bar. I snapped off a piece and popped it into my mouth.

I could taste the purity of the dairy milk, even the delicate cacao butter. It was smooth, creamy, and wonderful.

My taste buds were tasting again!

Properly.

As before.

Now I not only had my love back, I also had my chocolate back.

I brought three more bars, returned to the SUV, and we celebrated with Cadbury.

The next day, Ian, of course, went back to work, and I joined him.

"You're a beauty with a shovel," he said.

"Thanks to Luis."

"Thanks to Luis."

That night we made our plans:

I'd live in my father's house in Armadale, then sell it later in the year, before moving to the cottage after the wedding. I'd spend the rest of the spring digging on Skye with Ian and Jimmy, then spent most of the summer back in Manhattan, digging with Luis and the boys on Mondays, Wednesdays, and Fridays. The rest of the time, I'd help out Aunt Katie at Kinnell's Chocolates. Then, in the early fall, I'd return to Skye to make final wedding arrangements.

With a beautiful dress from Lord & Taylor.

A Princess Ball-Gown V-Neck Court-Train Satin

& Lace with a Ruffle.

Already, of course, I'd reconnected with the various chocolate companies, and I was soon back-on-track, with my usual tastings schedules in June and October.

In May, I also signed with Cadbury. I'd always wanted to work for them, but they already had an excellent taster, but then she decided to retire. I've always had a special spot for Cadbury, founded by the Quaker John Cadbury in 1824 in Birmingham, but now headquartered in not-too-far Uxbridge, London.

Jimmy, a longtime Cadbury enthusiast, was absolutely delighted. He was also delighted about the opening of the New Sult Inn in June on Macdougal Street. He not only got to visit New York again, but he got to hear Ian fiddling on opening night, and, for the opening week, he got to insult/compliment all the new patrons in the Village.

Until they found an old Scotsman in Brooklyn who could handle the job when Jimmy wasn't there.

Even though he was never quite as good as you-know-who.

Despite all the insults, there were no mishaps at the brand-new tavern, as once had happened on the Island of Skye.

With Rickie, Aunt Katie, the New Sult Inn, Kinnell's Chocolates, and the Westchester diggers, we had unbreakable ties to America and many reasons to return.

Regularly.

But the digging was *always* the priority.

Monday, Wednesday, and Friday.

What about that?

Why had "Monday, Wednesday, and Friday" popped into my mind when I made my little vow in the Inverness chapel? I have no idea. Maybe the saint liked chocolate, which didn't even exist in his lifetime, and he wanted me to do what my father had trained me to do. Maybe it was a way to give me more "alone" time with Jimmy, helping with his schooling. Maybe it was because I wasn't a generational digger like Ian, who'd followed his father, who'd followed his own father.

I have no idea, but I'm grateful.

At any rate, *all* love stories should end with a wedding, with a vow of permanent love.

Right, Jimmy?

So where to have it?

When Ian proposed last Christmas at Eilean Donan, I'd said we should marry the following Christmas. I had no idea if it was even appropriate. It just popped into my head. Like the three days of the week. At any rate, Fr. Buchanan approved of the idea, and the wedding itself was scheduled at his lovely stone church, St. Mary's on Skye.

But where to have the reception?

December weather in the Highlands can be tricky, as I learned last year. The Gulf Stream usually keeps the coastal temperatures somewhat reasonable, but one could never be sure. So Duntulm was out. Even if we arranged for a tent of some kind within the ruins, the wind on the cliffs might blow everyone into the sea.

So we chose Armadale, where the MacDonalds moved after leaving Duntulm in the 1700's. Armadale Castle is also a ruin, mostly still standing, and strikingly beautiful. Its 20,000-acre estate includes the Museum of the Isles, famous gardens, and the Stables Restaurant. All of which is a few miles from St. Mary's.

Besides, Armadale is the place where my father spent the last four years of his life.

It was also the place where Flora MacDonald, who'd once aided Bonnie Prince Charlie, was married on November 6, 1750.

Which delighted the Memory Boy.

So earlier today at St. Mary's, I said the two most important words in my life.

"I do."

Then I heard the other two most important:

"I do."

Then, as you well know, Jimmy, Fr. Buchanan said to my husband.

"Now you can kiss the bride."

Which he did, with his handsome best man, James MacBride, standing at his side, with my maid of honor standing right beside me, Rickie Moreno.

(Who will also be reading this narrative, who looked as beautiful as beautiful could be.)

Sr. Marie (Heather) was there, in the back of the

church, sitting with another temporarily-uncloistered sister. Unfortunately, they couldn't come to the reception, but the rest of the usual suspects were there.

In the Stables Restaurant.

Stone, oak-paneled wood, with lovely windows.

Sgt. Moreno had given me away.

Dr. Jack Cooper escorted Rickie, after ten months of pretty serious dating.

Matty Brooks brought Kimberly Sinclair, the "snowbunny" I'd first met (and liked) at Córdoba's in Manhattan.

My dear Aunt Katie.

Nicholas Palmer from St. Anthony's Cemetery.

Luis Flores, Carlos, and Fernando.

My "brother diggers," all spruced up, handsome as could be, escorted sweet Maria, Luis's sister.

Even Dr. MacAllister drove down from Inverness, saying he wanted to see if Ian was still "alive and kicking."

And now my wonderful Ian is singing my father's song and making me cry.

> *Bidh mo ghaol-sa dhi buan am feasda*
> *Air Eilean àluinn a' Cheò.*

Then singing those lines in English:

> *I will love my love forever and ever*
> *On the beautiful Island of Skye.*

When he finished, he nodded to the band, and they immediately played Anne Murray's "Can I Have This Dance (For The Rest Of My Life)," and we danced like we did last Christmas at Eilean Donan Castle, when he asked me to marry him.

Tomorrow, I'll give these scribblings to the Memory Boy. His long overdue, overlong, love story, with all its failings.

With all its inadequacies.

With its theme of love.

Then Ian and I will leave on our honeymoon to (where else?) New Jersey. To beautiful Cape May, which is perfectly beautiful in the summer, and just as beautiful in the dead of winter.

Then the Chocolate Princess and her Graveyard Knight intend to live happily ever after.

With Jimmy.

Working together.

As Fernando used to say:

"Gravediggers are never out of work."

William Baer is the award-winning author of more than thirty books including the Jack Colt mystery series *New Jersey Noir*, the Deirdre Flanagan mystery series, *Companion*, *Advocatus Diaboli*, *Times Square and Other Stories*, *Classic American Films*, and *One-and-Twenty Tales*. A graduate of Rutgers, NYU, South Carolina, the Johns Hopkins Writing Seminars, and USC Cinema, he's been the recipient of a Guggenheim Fellowship, a Fulbright (Portugal), an NEA fellowship in fiction, and the Jack Nicholson Screenwriting Award. He lives happily in a log cabin in the lake region of north New Jersey.